Hardcover ISBN 979-8-9887923-5-2
Paperback ISBN 979-8-9887923-4-5
eBook ISBN 979-8-9887923-3-8

Cover design: R.L.Rocole
Photo: Shutterstock, artist, Inna Sinano
Editor: Belle Manuel Editorial Service

Readers be advised.

This book is a work of fiction. Names, characters, places, and incidents are the product of the authors imagination or are used fictitiously. Any resemblance to actual events or persons, living or dead is coincidental.

This book contains strong language, adult content, violence, attempted rape and torture, intended for a mature audience.

To Jeffrey

Behold the steady midnight breeze
which ebbs and flows with perfect ease
A never-ending rhythmic flow
That only strengthens as you go

Stay strong and steady, little one.

Daughter Of Bathory

C.L. Kowalchuk

Chapter 1.

Rats are returning to the castle. Cold wind from the north is driving them indoors to escape the worst of the impending storm. A giant black rat is staring straight at me when I wake up. My groan of disgust is enough to send him scurrying under my bed with a squeak of protest.

My eyelids are still heavy and I am tempted to sink back into the safety of my dreams, but it is useless. I hear him under there now, along with many others. They are waiting for me to drop a morsel of food for them.

They may be hungry, but so am I, and there isn't a single crumb to offer.

Staring at the ceiling, I sigh. There is no use trying to fall back asleep. The squeaks are impossible to ignore now that I know they are there.

As the rodents search for crumbs, I pull the blanket tighter around my body, hoping the thin fabric is enough to deter their hungry advances. When winter is in full swing, they will become desperate for food. Their desperation makes them dangerous. These Slovakian winters are not for the faint of heart. Only the strong will survive.

On several occasions I have awoken to them gnawing on the hem of my dress, seeking nourishment from the only thing left edible in this section of the castle. Me.

I wonder, not for the first time, what it would feel like to be eaten alive by these rodents. Would it be a long, drawn-out process when I eventually succumb to infection? Or would their sharp teeth hit a vital source of blood, letting me bleed out quickly? That option seems preferable to spending another winter in this frozen prison.

Last year, I was certain the brutal winter would claim me in its passage. The toes on my left foot tingle from the sickly shade of purple they had turned during the worst of the cold. A swift death of being eaten alive does not seem as daunting when faced with the alternative of remaining here another year.

That is a consideration for another day, however. Today, the rats are merely a nuisance and keep their scavenging efforts to the floor.

I squeeze my eyes shut again, ignoring the horrors that surround me for one more brief moment.

A scream comes from the castle above me. It is high-pitched and feminine. A woman, by the sound of it. They usually are. My mother has a taste for them.

Resignedly, I open my eyes and look at the barred window, wishing there was some way to help her. But I push that thought away quickly.

I can no more save her than I can save myself.

The only mercy she can hope for is for death to come quickly. However, if my mother is in a foul mood, she can make the pain last hours—even days.

The frequent screams make it impossible to stay asleep at night, so I sleep during the day. I can never be sure what to expect during those dark hours and prefer to keep my wits about me.

Some nights, it is quiet. But some nights, it is an endless barrage of echoing cries. Those sounds haunt me long after the unfortunate souls have stopped their suffering. Either way, it is my habit now to sleep only during the day when I know all will be silent.

The fading light through the window tells me the sun has just begun its descent over the horizon. A kaleidoscope of orange and yellows slides down the wall slowly, creating the illusion of warmth upon the stark grey walls.

I sit up and stretch my arms high over my head, removing the last remnants of sleep from my body. A mixture of pain and relief meets my aching back as I arch backward, trying to alleviate the stiffness. After years of sleeping in an uncomfortable bed, one would think my body would adjust, but my muscles still protest every time I wake up.

A cloud of dust billows into the air as I swing my feet off over the side of the bed and stomp my feet loudly on the dirt floor. This proves effective in sending the rodents scampering off through the gap at the base of the door. Once they are gone, I stand to wash with the water set out for me. The floor is ice cold, and I tiptoe across the brick to slip on my shoes. A shiver slides up my arms, and I have to force myself not to jump back under my covers.

A handful of cool water helps remove the last sleep from my eyes, and I blink rapidly to remove the droplets from my vision.

I try to smooth out the tangles in my hair before giving up and fastening a loose braid at the base of my neck. With only the waters diluted reflection I can't see myself clearly, but it hardly matters if my hair is a mess. I rarely see anyone for days on end.

A servant girl is the only person who ever visits my cell when she delivers fresh water and a single meal. Each day is the same. I receive one bucket of water, a slice of plain bread, and a bowl of lukewarm soup. If I am lucky, she also brings an armful of firewood, but that is only on the coldest nights.

A wood stove in the corner barely puts out enough heat to warm my hands, let alone the entire cell. The porous brick soaks the heat up like a sponge, leaving me shivering under my blanket.

In winter, I often fall asleep next to the stove only to find the fire barely more than embers when I wake. It is never enough, but I am grateful for the small comfort. Without it, I would have never survived this long.

The water I receive is used for both drinking and bathing. The latter of which I do just before the servant arrives to keep the water clean as long as possible.

The water's surface is clear enough to act as a mirror and I am repulsed by the reflection staring back at me.

I do not have an unpleasant-looking face.

With my almond-shaped brown eyes and straight black hair, I would even go so far as to say I am attractive. Beautiful even. At least from what I can see in the diluted reflection.

It is what my face represents that repulses me. It is the only thing that has kept me alive for this long and keeps me a prisoner in this frozen hellscape.

I have the face of my father. The only man my mother ever loved. I suppose I should be grateful she has kept me alive this long when she has disposed of others so quickly, but I feel only hatred.

Hatred towards her and hatred towards this life she has exiled me to.

The anger threatens to consume me as I gaze at the crumbling brick and cracked ceiling. Not even an animal could thrive under these sorts of conditions.

I count backward, as I have done a thousand times before. My anger must always stay in check. The rage inside me needs to stay below the surface. It can never show on my face when I am in her presence.

In the past, I would throw myself at the walls, screaming and crying in frustration. The blood trailing down my fingers helped bring me back from the brink of madness. It felt good to feel something, even if it was pain, but those bouts of anger soon faded.

As I grew older, I found another way to ground myself. Now, I thrive on control. It is my key to freedom. Anger and sadness will get me nowhere. Submission is the card I need to play. At least for now. Until my chance of freedom comes.

I cannot spend another winter here. There must be a way out, even if it is through my death, either at my mother's hands or my own. I will escape this cell one way or another.

This solitude is driving me mad, one day at a time. I want to feel alive and exist outside these four walls.

I want to be free.

Smoothing out the wrinkles of my tattered gown, I sit on the bed's edge while awaiting the guard's arrival. He does not come every day. Only on the days my mother wishes to see me. But after years of observing her moods, I know her well enough to know that today will be one of those days. She is a creature of habit, and the full moon peeking above the horizon tells me everything I need to know.

She will want to see my face today.

My suppositions are confirmed when I hear the guard walking down the stone corridor. I count his footsteps and know the exact moment he steps outside my door. He raps loudly on the door three times—the same as every other time.

"Mask," he bellows.

His voice is muffled by the thick iron, but it sends me shooting off the bed with a grin. Excitement bubbles up in my stomach as I walk to the door and reach for the porcelain mask that hangs on a hook.

For a moment, my excitement is dampened by the mask, but I push down the anxiety and place the confining veil over my face. It is meant to shield my face from those who might envy it. At least, that is what my mother tells me.

But I know the truth.

It is her selfishness that keeps me locked away. She is the only one allowed to gaze upon my face under the threat of death. Only one other person in the last nine years has seen me without the mask. That person is now dead.

A doctor was brought to my cell to help bring me back from the brink of death. The cold weather caused a cough, which quickly turned severe. I sat gasping for breath as he listened to my lungs and placed a hand against my skin to check for a fever. After a horrible coughing fit, he removed the mask from my face so I could gather a full breath. After he prescribed a poultice and herbal concoction for my fever, he was beaten to death a few feet from my cell.

No one disregards my mother's orders. It is not tolerated.

My fingers tremble as I tie the mask in place with a crimson ribbon, knotting it twice to make sure it does not come undone.

With a deep breath, I return his knock, notifying the guard that I am ready. My heart thunders in my chest as he slides the bolt aside.

The hinges let out a groan of protest as he swings the door open and ushers me forward.

The other sections of the castle are usually off limits to me and I can't help but shiver in anticipation before stepping out of my cell.

I never know what to expect during visits with my mother. Her moods are unpredictable and range from soft murmurs of admiration to wild outbursts that leave me trembling in fear.

My erratic breathing echoes inside the mask, and I try to slow my breaths and control my racing heart. The holes cut into the eyes of the mask are large enough that I have an unobstructed view of my surroundings. I gaze around, drinking in every detail as if it is the first time.

The same guard who has accompanied me on my last few outings stands before me. He smells strongly of old whiskey and sways on his feet as he stares at me with red-rimmed eyes.

His name is Reginald.

I learned this from the numerous women he has brought down here at night. They moan and yell out his name while he fucks them in the cell across from me.

"Harder, Reginald," they scream. Or, "Ow Reginald, you are hurting me." He seems to go through phases. It's either too hard or too soft, but never just right. Perhaps it depends on the woman. Maybe some like it harder, while some like to be coddled. I may never know the answer.

I don't know what could be so pleasurable, but they seem to enjoy it. To me, it sounds like Reginald is doing nothing more than rutting like an animal and grunting obscenities while he bangs them against the wall. He calls them filthy whores and smacks their bare skin with his dirty hands. I can't imagine deriving pleasure from this odious man.

Although, a hidden part of me does wonder what it would be like to have a man touch me. Not Reginald, of course, but a man whom I care for. A man who isn't vulgar and hurling insults when he's inside me.

On the occasions when I let my mind wander to such possibilities, a ball of heat gathers in my stomach, and a pulse begins between my thighs. It is excruciating and delicious in equal measure. I have let my hand wander beneath my skirt and touch the place where the sensitive skin is flaming hot and wet with desire.

It would mean a severe punishment if anyone found out that I pleasured myself in such a way, but the need to release that pent-up desire is worth the risk of being caught.

Reginald clears his throat, and I bring my attention back to him.

He is what some women might consider ruggedly attractive. His square jaw and large frame are pleasant enough, but I would rather cut off my arm than let him touch me.

A dark glint enters his eyes as he gazes up and down my body. He licks his lips as if he is about to partake in a delicious meal. Bile rises in my throat as his trousers begin to bulge, showing off his arousal. No amount of attractiveness can hide the dark soul hiding under the surface of this man.

It feels like insects are crawling all over my skin while he continues to leer at my curves, and a lascivious grin crosses his face. I do not allow myself to react. I do not want to make a scene today of all days. Confrontation will only lead to punishment, and I will once again be confined to my room.

Reginald's belt hangs low on his hips, and he leans to one side with an arrogant pose.

"You're a good girl, now, aren't you, Pet," he says, showing teeth too big for his mouth. He is a man of few words unless his cock is involved. Then he is a regular old chatterbox.

Dirty bastard.

I say nothing, knowing I am not allowed to converse with anyone except my mother. I must follow the rules. And there are many rules. The clang of handcuffs sounds loud in the empty hall as he repositions his trousers, and I hold up my hands automatically, knowing what comes next.

He pulls the handcuffs off his belt and clasps them tightly to my wrists. Metal bites into my skin when he squeezes them harder than usual with a smirk. Why he thinks I need handcuffs is a mystery. What am I going to do?

Run off into the wilderness in the middle of the night?

He is easily twice my size, and it wouldn't take him long to overpower me. This is just how he likes to show his dominance. He is telling me he controls me without uttering a single word.

He turns me towards the corridor and presses his body up against me. His hand moves over my ribcage as he holds me in place.

Oh, really nice. Since when has frisking become part of our routine?

My teeth nearly crack with the effort it takes to keep my mouth shut as he moves each massive palm over my breasts and grasps them so tightly, I nearly cry out.

His hand wanders back down to circle my waist, and every instinct inside me tells me to run, but he holds me fast against him. I contemplate screaming to stop his disgusting advances. Not that screaming will be much help. This section of the castle is so remote no one would hear my pleas for help.

He inhales deeply, and I realize, with disgust, he is smelling a tendril of my hair.

He groans and steps away, thankfully putting distance between me and his rising cock.

"Soon, girl," he says resignedly, before making his way down the corridor.

I chance one more look back towards my room, which is both my solitude and my prison. This night may very well end in disaster. At least when I'm inside my cell, everything is predictable. Boredom. Cold. Rats. Hunger. Repeat. But out here, anything goes. Reginald is not the only threat I will face tonight.

When dealing with my mother, nothing can be certain. I don't know why that prospect both terrifies and excites me. Perhaps because the unknown is better than nothingness.

I am tired of simply existing. If I must endure another winter of bitter cold, shivering under the pathetic excuse of a blanket, madness will soon claim me.

This will be the year when the tiny flicker of life inside me either bursts into flames or is entirely extinguished, leaving a hollow shell in my place.

This recurring nightmare of solitude cannot go on. I will not allow it. What is the worst that can happen? She will kill me? That is a chance I have to take. I must cling to my only hope, that she will not kill the only thing remaining of the man she once loved. My demise would mean losing my face. This perfectly replicated façade of her dead lover.

I may mean nothing to her, but my face surely does.

Chapter 2.

We pass several empty cells on our way out of the dungeon. The iron doors are open wide, inviting anyone brave enough to peek inside and see what remains of the previous occupants.

A centipede, which must be nearly a foot long, crosses the path in front of us, traversing a path into one of the cells where a long-forgotten corpse is lying in a heap on the floor. The insect climbs the skeletal remains and disappears into the head before reemerging moments later from its mouth. Perhaps one day I will end up in the same state as that corpse. Alone and rotting in a cell with no one to keep me company except rodents and centipedes. The latter of which may take up residency inside my skull.

The guard lets out an annoyed yell for me to continue, and I walk quickly to where he is standing near the entrance.

The sight of the night sky behind him causes me to quicken my pace. There is no door to separate the dungeon's entrance from the outside world, and I follow the guard out into the night, crossing over the threshold with a sigh of relief.

The stars are magnificent in the black expanse of never-ending sky. A million twinkling orbs shine down at me from above, winking as I stare at them from behind the confines mask. Tears prick the corners of my eyes as I process the enormity of its beauty.

Finding the brightest star, I squeeze my eyes shut and make a wish.

I wish for freedom. I want to rip this horrid mask off my face and run into the surrounding woods, never to lay eyes on this castle or the occupants again.

Reginald pushes me forward roughly as his impatience with my distraction grows.

Whirling around, I pierce him with my most intimidating stare, but he sneers at my attempt and saunters by me. His shoulder knocks into me as he passes.

My temper begs to release a string of curse words that would put a sailor to shame, but I swallow the insults burning on my tongue. Not tonight. I must remain in control. At least for now.

The dungeon is located on the south side of the castle. It is situated below the imposing gothic-style structure with no way to gain access except to traverse the winding staircase that hugs the building's exterior. We begin climbing the stairs, and Reginald rests several times to catch his breath. Apparently, the alcohol he consumed earlier makes him tire easily.

Rotting leaves cover the rarely used steps, hiding crumbling brick and icy patches beneath. I choose my footing carefully, knowing that one misstep will make me tumble back to the bottom. My life is already miserable enough without adding a broken bone or two to the mix. Reginald pitches forward as his foot catches a slick spot but he manages to right himself before falling. He glares back at me as if this is somehow all my fault. Did I put that ice there? No, I did not. Keep moving asshole.

The thought of his broken body lying at the bottom of the stairs is entirely too appealing, and I wonder how difficult an accident would be to orchestrate. Probably not difficult at all by the smell of him. He would probably tip over like a leaf in the wind if I gave him a gentle nudge. I chuckle, and that earns me another glare.

I contemplate all the ways I could manage to upset his footing but brush the thought away. Fortunately for Reginald, I am no murderer.

So, instead of acting out my wayward fantasy, I follow behind him, stopping when he stops and ascending at an increasingly slow pace.

A dense forest surrounds the castle, and small animals dart through the trees as darkness closes in around us. A flash of something larger catches my attention in the foliage to my left.

A smile curls up the corners of my mouth at the sight of ebony fur. It is my only friend. The wolf.

I first met him when I was eleven years old. I was sitting in the corner of my cell, crying my little eyes out with snot running down my face. A sound from outside my window caught my attention, and I quieted my cries to focus on where the noise was coming from.

Pulling a wooden chair up to the base of the window, I peered over the edge and saw a small black wolf cub pawing at the wall, as if he were trying to climb it. He yipped several times and jumped up, trying to reach what was on the other side.

Standing on my tiptoes, I reached over the edge of the window and held my hand outside to him. The sight of my hand poking through the window must have startled him, and he cocked his head to the side, trying to figure out what in the world to do now.

His nose was only a few inches from my hand, but neither of us could extend our bodies further to close the distance between us. So, he reared back and jumped up, licking my fingers.

He came back frequently, and as the years progressed and as we both grew, we were able to reach each other through the window. My only comfort in this life is running my fingers through his coarse fur as I pour out every thought to him. His light brown eyes are a startling contrast to his dark fur and give him an almost mythical quality. He is my only companion in this isolated world, and without him, I fear I would not have survived this long. I may have already chosen to give up.

The presence of other people always startles him, and he quickly retreats into the trees at the first sound of human intervention. Even now, I know he is nearby, but he won't show himself until everyone else has gone away and all is quiet in the woods again.

We begin to climb the stairs again, but I can feel the wolf's eyes on me, and it makes me feel safer knowing he is watching.

As we continue upwards, my breath comes out in thick, white puffs, and I rub my hands together to help bring warmth back into my cold limbs. My legs felt comfortably warm from the exertion but my fingers and the tip of my nose are icy cold.

Finally, we reach the top of the hill, and the guard places a hand on a nearby wall as he pulls in deep breaths. He mumbles something under his breath that sounds like a string of expletives, and I stifle a laugh at his obvious discomfort.

We enter the castle through the servant's entrance and navigate through the bustling kitchen as people scurry about, preparing for dinner. Several of them peer at me from the corners of their eyes before turning away quickly. No one wants to be caught staring.

The smells coming from the stove are enough to make my mouth water, and a loud grumble escapes my stomach. I haven't eaten yet today, and the gnawing ache that was present earlier turns into a painful clench at the sight of the delectable meal.

Blueberry pie and apple cobbler are set out on a table to cool, and a giant hog turns on a spit over the open fireplace.

The fire crackles as grease from the pig drips into the flames. A wave of bile begins to rise in my throat from the sickening ache that is building in my empty stomach. My fingers itch to reach out and grab a biscuit as we pass by them. Instead, I keep my shackled hands clasped tightly together and my head held high.

Maintaining the illusion of a dutiful daughter is of the utmost importance, and it won't do to have someone accuse me of being a thief. Thankfully, before I can embarrass myself by throwing myself on the food and devouring it, we exit the kitchen. I take a deep breath and push down the hunger as the scents disappear behind us.

These richly tapestried walls and gleaming floors are a stark contrast to my own pitiful accommodations. I bite back the anger that threatens to emerge in the face of all this finery. It's not like I even care about the splendor. It's just the thought that one gold ornament adorning the strategically placed side tables would be enough for me to live a simple life far away from here.

I often daydream about all the adventures that await me, separated only by the iron door cell. But tonight, I will focus on what is ahead instead of what could be.

It will do me no good to get angry before the night has even begun.

A long corridor, lit on each side by wall sconces, leads to a chamber where the servants will prepare me before I am allowed to see my mother. She will expect nothing less than perfection. If even one hair is out of place, someone's head will roll for the oversight.

When we reach our destination, I face Reginald so he can remove my handcuffs, which he does without uttering a sound. We are in my mother's domain now, and he won't risk his filthy advances while she might overhear.

A servant girl opens the door with her head bowed demurely, and she ushers me inside.

A fireplace is lit on the opposite wall, and the room's warmth immediately begins to thaw my frozen skin. I almost sigh at the sight of the steaming bathtub which is set in the middle of the room, just waiting for me to sink into it.

Another servant stands beside the tub, and I walk to her before turning to face the opposite wall.

Both women are dressed in long black dresses and cloaks with their hair pinned in a severe bun at the base of their necks. Not a hint of makeup or frivolities is allowed for my mother's maidservants.

Every woman who resides here is often downright haggard in appearance. Elizabeth would never allow anyone to outshine her legendary beauty.

These women have never told me their names, and I have not asked. Conversation is forbidden between us, but I have secretly named them Olivia and Rebecca.

Olivia has freckles and red hair hidden away behind a black cap. Her face is pleasant enough except for the puckered burn scar on her right cheek. It was my mother's way of ensuring her wholesome face would never garner more attention than her own.

She is the one who brings the food and water to my room every day. Her expressive green eyes show every emotion, and they will undoubtedly get her in trouble one day when she betrays too much.

Even now, her eyes search my body for signs of injury, and her brows rise, asking without words if I am alright. The reason behind her kindness is a mystery, but I am thankful every time she extends a bit of warmth to me. It reminds me that there are people in this world who aren't entirely horrid after all.

She sneaks bits of treats onto my plate when no one is looking and blankets appear out of nowhere on the coldest nights. Once, an entire piece of apple pie appeared alongside my daily ration of bread and soup. I ate that pie painfully slow, wanting the experience to last forever. The way that sugary treat melted on my tongue is an experience I will never forget.

Rebecca is much shorter, with a plain face and haunted brown eyes. She reminds me of a scared mouse and jumps anytime the slightest noise is made. I'm sure the look of constant fear in her eyes is my mother's doing, but she would do well to hide it. Mother loves to prey on fear.

Everyone who works here is indebted to my mother in some way. Either to pay off their debt or a family member's. Once they have paid their dues, they are free to leave. But I have never seen anyone fulfill their obligation. Usually, they vanish after a year or two of service, never to be seen again.

Olivia undresses me, removing my cloak and dress, while Rebecca removes my shoes, slipping the tattered fabric from my feet. A clean dress has already been set out on a chair beside the tub, and a fresh set of shoes is placed below it.

The only thing that remains in place is my mask. They are not allowed to remove it.

When undressed, I gingerly place one foot into the hot bath water. A shiver of delight travels up my body, and my skin breaks out in goosebumps as the delicious warmth seeps into my limbs. I sink into the water, not caring when pins and needles race up my limbs from the shock of the hot water.

Both women begin the process of scrubbing the dirt from my body and washing my hair. I focus on the bubbles floating above the water and touch one, smiling as it pops under my finger.

Moments of joy are so scarce that even the sight of a tiny bubble popping is enough to make me smile. How pathetic is that? A sad, pathetic, lonely existence. But I won't dwell on that now. I will simply enjoy this fleeting moment.

The water turns murky as my hair is rinsed, and my skin begins to feel raw from the scrubbing efforts of the women. I can't blame them for being extra thorough. I wouldn't want to be on the receiving end of my mother's wrath if she notices a missed spot of dirt.

Rebecca holds up a robe for me, and with a resigned sigh, I stand up. The water runs down my body, and I already miss the warmth as it trickles down my skin. I step out onto the cold floor, and she wraps the thick fabric around me before clinching a belt around my waist.

She leads me to a vanity table, where I wait for the remainder of the preparations to begin. The mirror has been removed, so I cannot look at myself, but I wouldn't want to see the reflection anyway. This mask is the only thing that would stare back at me, and I have no desire to see my eyes peering out through the oval holes.

I close my eyes as they brush through my tangled hair and rub lotion on my skin. I focus on the feelings that so many others may take for granted. The strands of the hairbrush stroking against my scalp rhythmically. The feelings of actual physical contact as hands stroke up and down my arms and legs, smoothing the thick lotion into my skin. The soft fabric beneath my fingers as my thumb strokes the velvet bathrobe.

Finally, the women finish their work and turn away from me so I can finish the last part myself.

I remove the mask and turn to a basin of water and soap on the vanity. Dipping a cloth into the water, I wipe my face with soapy water and rinse my skin clean. I dry it with a different cloth before picking up a small handheld mirror, barely bigger than my palm.

My eyes seem different than the last time I sat here. They look older than they ever have before. Despair has begun to cause lines to form at the corners of my eyes, even though I am barely an adult. But even with the added hint of despair, there is no denying that a hidden spark still lies beneath the sadness. I wonder briefly if this will be the year that spark gets snuffed out or bursts into a fiery inferno.

Sighing, I put the mirror down, satisfied that my face is clean enough to pass my mother's inspection. Fastening the mask back in place, I stand and turn so the finishing touches can be applied.

The women dress me in a plain black dress and cloak which they fasten with a dragon pendant. The dragon has its tail wrapped around itself into a circle and a red ruby in place of its eye. It is an expensive piece and will be removed before they return me to the dungeon, but for now, I hold my head high and act like a high-born daughter Mother expects me to be.

I walk to a door on the opposite side of the room. Not the same door from which I entered, but a door that leads to my next destination. My mother's bed chamber. Taking a deep breath, I open the door and step over the threshold.

I turn and make eye contact with Olivia. Her eyes tell me just how worried she is for me tonight. She closes the door with one last haunted look and locks me inside.

Chapter 3.

The door does not lead directly to her room. I must first pass through a corridor that seems to go on for an eternity. The narrow hall is lit by wall sconces, creating long shadows and the illusion of hidden figures behind each turn.

This passageway is a singular path forward with no other rooms branching off. However, it feels more like a maze with all the corners and bends. I have walked this path so often that I could walk the length of it blindfolded.

I know that my mother's inner sanctum is around the next bend, only ten paces ahead. The place where no rules apply to her dark appetite and all her wildest fantasies come true. My mother, Elizabeth Bathory, has rightly earned her title as the Blood Countess.

I walk to her door, making my footsteps as quiet as possible. Placing my ear against the thick wooden door, I hold my breath and listen, trying to learn what kind of mood my mother is in tonight.

All is quiet within, which makes me more nervous than the loud shattering of ceramic I was greeted with last time. At least then, I knew what to expect.

Quiet Elizabeth can be the most dangerous of all.

Taking a deep breath, I raise my hand and stand up taller. *Well, here goes nothing.*

I knock on the door three times and wait for her to bid me enter.

When a full minute passes, I grow confused. *Should I knock again? Perhaps she didn't hear me.* But just as I am about to knock a second time, a loud, guttural scream comes from the other side of the door.

I take a few steps backward, never once taking my eyes off the door. Perhaps I should run and make my escape before it is too late. Another scream tears through the air, and my hand flies to my throat, keeping in my own shriek of terror before it has a chance to escape.

Before I can decide whether fleeing or staying would be the wiser option, the door to her bedroom is thrown open. There, in all her glory, is my mother, streaked from head to toe in blood.

I know better than to cry out, but it takes all my willpower not to hurl up the contents of my stomach as the stench of blood hits me. The sickly copper smell is so strong I can taste it.

No, that can't be right, I think in confusion. I can actually taste blood. Then, I realize I am biting the inside of my cheek to keep from screaming, and the blood is my own.

"Anastasia, darling, come in please," Mother says with her usual velvety voice. She holds her arms out as if inviting me in for a cup of tea.

She seems not to care that streaks of red cover her from elbow to wrist. Or that her dress has crimson droplets sprayed across her bodice, extending up one side of her chin.

No. It could be any other mother greeting her daughter, waiting for a peck on each cheek and motherly embrace.

Swallowing down my bile, I force my mind away from the depravity and walk into her waiting arms. She is not a patient woman, and if I stall even a moment, it could turn the entire evening into a nightmare.

Wrapping her arms around me, she squeezes my shoulders, and the tips of her nails dig into my flesh as she holds onto me tighter than usual.

Something is wrong. I can sense it. Her excitement is a tangible emotion, and I can almost see the sparks of energy exploding beneath her skin.

When she finally steps back, she holds me at arm's length and rubs her hands up and down my arms with a maniacal gleam in her eye. I am careful to keep my expression blank, even though it is hidden behind my mask. Even a flinch or grimace might be enough to set off an explosion with her in this heightened state of angst.

"Come, daughter, let us sit by the fireplace and talk."

A trickle of fear winds its way around my heart. Talk? She has never once wanted me to talk in all my visits here. Silence is always required whenever in her presence.

The air is warm when I enter her bedroom, thanks to the roaring fireplace against the back wall. The goosebumps on my arms relax as the heat spreads across my body.

Her room is lavishly decorated with deep red and golden accents, creating a deliciously inviting atmosphere. Settees with overstuffed pillows and fur throws are sprinkled throughout the room, inviting the occupants to indulge in the opulence.

A large painting hanging just above the fireplace is the focal point for the entire room and demands your attention. It shows my mother lying on a settee with her head thrown back and a look of utter rapture on her face. Her eyes are squeezed shut, and her hand is between her thighs. Although the hand is hidden behind the fabric of her gown, one doesn't need to guess too hard about what she is doing.

Even if that isn't enough to draw you into the painted scene, what is in her other hand truly draws your attention. In her fist, grasped tightly by the crown of his hair, is a man's decapitated head. A look of astonishment is written across his pale face as if he can't believe he is truly dead. His mouth is wide open, waiting to release a scream that will never come.

The eyes of the deceased man seem to follow me as I make my way over to a chair.

My body only makes it halfway to my seated position before I freeze in place. On the other side of the room, propped up in a chair, is the source of the earlier scream.

A young woman is sitting across from me, supported by the curvature of a wingback chair. Her eyes are wide open, but the vacant look in her gaze tells me she has already left this world for a place much less cruel.

Blood drips from several bite marks across her arms, and a wet spot between her thighs indicates she soiled herself at some point. Whether she lost her bowels before or after death, I can only guess.

But that is not what caused the coppery tang which fills the room. It is the slice across her neck that sealed her fate to the afterlife. No blood soils her dress from the wound, however.

No. That would be a waste.

A ceramic pot sitting next to the chair is filled with her lifeblood to be used later.

Blood is the one thing my mother craves above all else. She believes it is the nectar of youth and brushes it over her skin in an effort to retain her youthful appearance. She even goes so far as to bathe her entire body in it if sources are plentiful enough.

I have tried to control my reaction to blood, but it brings out an uncontrolled visceral response that cannot be avoided. Just the smell of it makes me physically ill. Never mind the sight of it, which compounds the effect tenfold.

If I don't breathe in through my nose or look in the direction of the dead girl maybe it won't be so bad. I focus on my breathing and take small, measured breaths through my mouth.

I unfreeze from my half-sitting position and fully lower myself to my seat, trying to wish away the image of the girl's sightless eyes.

My mother circles me like a vulture preparing to swoop down and devour its meal. She stops behind me and strokes my shoulders with a caress so gentle I can barely feel it. Her fingers barely make contact with my skin, and the sensation causes goosebumps to break out across my flesh.

"Take off your mask, darling," she whispers in my ear.

With practiced ease, I untie the ribbon and place the mask on my lap as Mother walks around to stand in front of me. The effort to keep my face neutral is taking its toll on me. A muscle twitches in my eye and I pray she doesn't notice.

"My beautiful Anastasia. No other face can compare to yours," she says, stroking the back of her hand down my cheek. "And now we can finally be together."

"What?" I ask, confused, before catching myself and returning to my stoic position.

"It is all right, my dear. You can speak freely now. I will allow it. You see," she says, kneeling before me and looking me directly in the eye, "My husband, Ferenc, has died and left me all alone to rule these lands."

Shock steals my voice even though I have a dozen questions. Out of all the things she could have told me, this is the most unexpected.

"Don't you see? We can be together now. He is the one who kept you locked away in that cell for all these years. It was his jealousy that demanded you always stay out of sight. But now... well, now. I can finally be reunited with my one true love. Your father."

"Reunited?" I ask, more confused than ever. "But how?"

She sighs as if talking to a silly child and shakes her head. "My dear, it is your face and the blood flowing through your veins that has been your salvation. The reason for keeping you alive all these years."

She walks to a side table and uncorks a bottle of wine. Two crystal goblets are arranged on a tray, and she pours them half full of the crimson liquid. She carries them over and hands me one of the glasses. Not knowing what else to do, I accept it and take a sip before grimacing at the bitter taste of the dry wine.

I have never tasted wine, but expected it to be sweeter than this. I take another sip, not wanting to offend her, and the second sip goes down easier than the first.

"Let us celebrate. Here is to the future, and all that shall come to pass," she says, holding her cup into the air before taking a long drink and draining her cup.

The side door opens and Mother's advisor, Magda steps inside the room, holding a leather bag in her arms. Her appearance can, at best, be described as ancient, if I am being polite, and haggard if I am not.

Her face is weathered, with prominent cheekbones pulled tightly over skeletal bones. Her grey hair is woven into a long braid which falls to the middle of her back. It shows only hints of the deep black color it must have once been. Tiny bones are woven throughout her hair and attached to her cloak. They rattle together as she walks, lending another unsettling element to the already macabre environment.

"Magda, you are just in time. Anastasia and I were just celebrating the good news."

Magda cackles and takes several items out of the leather bag, laying them on a side table. One of the items is a dagger with a fierce sharp tip, and I swallow down the fear that blooms in my chest.

"It's about time that old bastard died. Now our plans can begin in earnest," she says, in a voice tarnished with age.

"What plans?" I ask.

"You haven't told her yet?" Magda asks, clucking her tongue. "We need her to be compliant, Elizabeth. This information will take time to sink in."

Sweat breaks out beneath my armpits. "Compliant?"

"Yes, dear. Have another sip of your wine," Mother says, smiling down at me.

Mother's too-sweet words suddenly seems foreboding. Something is wrong. Nausea begins to turn in my stomach, and I take a deep breath through my nose to quell it but immediately realize my mistake. The coppery scent of blood flows in my nose instead of the fresh air I desperately crave. I look to the side door, wondering what my chances are of escaping without being detained, but realize that the chances are slim, if any.

Instead of cowering in my chair, I sit tall and face what is coming head-on.

"Tell me, Mother. What exactly does this plan of yours involve?"

She saunters over to the items Magda brought and picks up the dagger. Placing a finger over the tip, she pierces her skin just enough to allow a single drop of blood to escape. She puts the knife back on the table and licks the drop of blood, closing her eyes and moaning in delight at the taste.

"Well, daughter, Magda has found a way to bring your father back to life."

My skepticism must be evident because she lifts her eyebrows and goes on.

"It is true. She has located his spirit in the afterlife and has the means to return it to his mortal body."

"But his mortal body is gone. After all this time, surely all that remains is bones."

"Yes," Magda laughs. "But any mortal body with his blood will do."

The confusion falls from my face, replaced with icy fear. "You mean me. My body."

"You finally understand," Mother says. "You see, that is why I kept you alive all these years. You are the vessel that will return my love to me. It must be fate that your features so resemble his own. It will be just like it was before he died. I kept your face hidden all these years so no one would know the truth about who he truly is. We can finally live together without the burden of our pasts weighing us down. We will be free to love each other once again."

The entire scenario seems surreal, and I blink several times, trying to process what she has just told me. This is madness. It will never work.

Magda is rummaging through the items on the table and begins chanting quietly. The words willing, and virgin are the only things I can understand from her ramblings, and I fight to keep my fear at bay.

"I will never be willing for something like this," I say, only realizing my mistake after the words are out in the open.

Mother's icy stare zeroes in on my face.

Oh shit.

She walks towards me with unnerving determination written on her face and grabs the front of my dress.

"You will abide, dear girl, or I will make death seem a preferable choice to what I have in store for you if you deny me this."

Magda picks up a glass vial from the table and holds it up for me to see. A blue swirl of incandescent light floats inside. The light ebbs and flows as if it is made of fluid matter.

"See how he begs to be let out," Magda whispers.

The light flickers inside the glass and becomes so bright I squint my eyes before it returns to the faint blue from moments ago.

My mouth drops open at the implication of what they have accomplished. I may have lived a very sheltered life, but can such magic indeed exist? If they can do something of this sort, might they actually succeed in transferring his soul into my body? The thought terrifies me, and I suddenly don't feel nearly as brave as I did moments ago in the face of such power.

Magda returns the glass jar to the table. She gazes at the blinking orb with undeniable admiration, like a mother might look at an infant.

Trailing a finger over the glass, a ghost of a smile crosses her lips. She sighs deeply before picking up the dagger and walking to the dead girl.

Her body blocks the girl from view, but the sound of the dagger cutting through flesh fills the room.

My stomach churns, and I swallow down the acid that begins to rise into my throat.

Don't you dare betray me, traitorous stomach.

No matter how often I practice controlling my features, my stomach is the one thing that will not obey my command. The queasy feeling continues to assault me as Magda goes about her work. When finally finished, she turns around and holds the girl's heart in her hands. Blood drops off her fingers and onto the floor, but she seems not to care. She steps over the droplets and places the heart into a stone mortar.

Her chanting fills the room as she sprinkles dried herbs over the heart and mashes it with a pestle. My breathing becomes erratic, and my heart thunders as my composure begins to crack. How in the hell am I going to get out of this mess?

When Magda has finished mixing all the ingredients, she hands the bowl to my mother, who takes it in reverently.

I begin to squirm in my chair when Magda walks to me and places her thumb on my forehead, streaking some of the blood onto my skin.

Her hand moves to the top of my head, and she begins chanting and gesturing wildly, waving her other arm and gyrating her hips in rhythm to a beat only she can hear. The bones on her clothing clatter together, cracking my composure, and a scream begins to build in my chest.

This has gone far enough. I can't just sit here while they prepare to take over my body with a spirit that may or may not be my father.

I knock Magda's hand away and stand off the chair. Compliance can only go so far. This is too much.

I back away, and they both seem surprised by my outburst, as if they genuinely thought I would go along with this madness.

"No," I say, trying to infuse strength into the single world.

"What did you say?" Mother spits out.

"I said no. I will not sit here while you perform this madness. I am more than a face and a body. I feel pain and fear, the same as any other person."

"Person?" she hisses, walking towards me. "You are not a person. You are only a vessel. One that I intend to dispose of if you don't do as I say."

"I will not."

"You little bitch," she says and strikes me across the face. The backhanded assault twists my head to the side, and even though I am trembling, I stand my ground. Looking her straight in the eye, I repeat, "No."

"Magda, bring the heart and dagger to me."

A wild glint comes into her eye, and a smile fit for the devil flashes across her face.

"We need her alive," Magda warns.

"I won't kill her. I only mean to persuade her."

Magda brings the requested items, and Mother grabs a handful of the bloody concoction in her hand.

"Eat it," she hisses, holding it up to my face.

The smell of the bloody mess is overwhelming. My stomach, which threatened to rebel earlier, makes another lurch of protest.

"Eat it," she screams, shaking with rage before pressing the mess to my lips. Even though my lips are pressed firmly closed, a bit of the pulp makes its way inside my mouth.

My mouth begins to water as I push against the urge to vomit. I know my efforts will be unsuccessful even before the acidic bile makes its way up my throat.

Pushing her hand away, I vomit down the front of her dress, retching as my stomach empties the rest of its contents.

She gazes down at the mess on her gown and back up at me with daggers shooting from her eyes.

"Look what you have done."

Before I have time to react, she grabs my hair and slams my head on the brick wall behind me. The force of the blow is excruciating, and stars swim in my vision. I shake my head to dislodge her grip, but it is useless. Her fingers are threaded through my hair in a steadfast grip.

Not satisfied with the outcome of her assault, she delivers another blow, and apparently, this one has the desired effect because the devilish smile is back on her face, and she comes in closer to whisper in my ear. “You will abide by my orders, Anastasia.”

Stars swim in my head and my vision begins to fade, engulfing me in darkness. The last thought that goes through my head as my world goes black is that this is not how I anticipated my night ending.

Chapter 4.

When I regain consciousness, the first thing that I feel is the searing pain in the back of my head. I touch my fingers gingerly to the sensitive area and find them come away sticky with blood.

A groan escapes my lips as I sit up and orient myself to my surroundings. Trying to keep out the light from my sensitive vision, I crack open one eyelid. My room surrounds me, and I let out a relieved sigh at the blessed silence.

At least my mother and her minion are nowhere to be found.

The room spins around me, and I sit against the wall while waiting for it to pass. Thoughts of the previous night begin to filter back into my mind while I wait for my dizziness to subside.

The blue orb. The wine. The blood. Oh god, the blood.

I push the thoughts away until I have more time to process everything. For now, I need water. My mouth feels like I swallowed sand and the throbbing in my head matches the beating of my heart.

When I stand up to gather water, I find the bucket missing. Confusion clouds my thoughts, and I search my mind for any indication of where it might be.

A memory comes back to me, just as I was fading into unconsciousness.

The voice of my mother saying, "Let's see how willing you become after a few days without food or water."

The words are, of course, followed by a hideous maniacal laugh.

"Well, shit. Now what?"

I have never been without water, and the prospect terrifies me. Food I can go without for days, but water. That is something I have never gone without.

I look around the room, trying to decide what to do. I notice snow has begun to fall outside. Walking to the window, I scoop up a handful of snowflakes. *I suppose this will have to do.*

I lick the icy flakes off my hand. They dissolve as soon as they touch my tongue, and after a few more handfuls, the parched ache in my throat begins to ease.

Next, I rip off a piece of my blanket, which is easy to accomplish since the fabric is threadbare in most areas. I wrap more snow inside it and place it against the back of my head, sighing when the cool fabric contacts my throbbing skull. After a few minutes, I pull the cloth away and see only a smudge of blood on it.

Thankfully, the bleeding seems to have stopped, and the aching is beginning to die down.

Wrapping myself in my blanket, I lay on my bed and shut my eyes.

The next few days are a mixture of sorrow and disbelief. The fact that my mother only kept me alive for her nefarious plot sits like a rock in my stomach. Even though she has treated me appallingly for the last nineteen years, a part of me secretly hoped she felt a tiny bit of love for me, which is why she has kept me alive all this time.

It never occurred to me that something like this was the reason. I fight away the thoughts that insist I should give in and let her have her way.

Even though I have so little to live for, a secret place in my heart still hopes that one day I might have a life far away from this wretched place.

As long as that flame of hope burns in my heart, I will fight.

To keep my mind off the hunger pains, I let my mind drift back to my childhood. The memories take me away from this misery for a few precious moments.

I haven't always lived in the dungeon of Castle Cachtice.

Glimpses of the nanny who cared for me are vague, but still present in my mind, like wisps of silk floating through the air. Memories of our beautiful manor house seem more like dreams than substantial memories. It seems so far removed from this life that it may have belonged to another person.

But I still remember.

The lilac flowers tickled my nose as I breathed in their fresh scent. The never-ending fields of fresh hay brushed against my legs as I ran through it. Most of all, I remember the animals.

A field behind the house was home to dozens of farm animals.

The silky feeling of the horse's nose is so vivid in my mind, I can nearly feel the warmth of its breath on my fingers.

When I managed to catch one, the chickens' soft feathers felt better than the finest fabrics.

The goats nibbling on the hem of my dress always caused me to giggle and play tug of war with the silly animals, even though it made my nanny cross when the goats tore off a piece and swallowed it.

These memories are precious to me, and I only bring them out when things are truly miserable. Perhaps it helps to keep the last spark of humanity inside me alight.

The first ten years of my life were filled with childish innocence, or perhaps it was ignorance. Either way. She was happy. Unlike the jaded woman I have become.

I miss that girl and her free spirit. But eventually, she found out how cruel this world can truly be. Mother would have left me there, in my private haven, but she bore no other children, and they became desperate for an heir.

A carriage came for me just after my tenth birthday.

The driver, a man named Borris with a shock of white hair, told me to pack my things. I was to move to the castle.

The excitement that bloomed in my chest was doused when I noticed my nanny wringing her hands.

"It's all right, my brave girl. Just remember to be good, and everything will be fine."

That statement did little to quell my confusion, but together, my nanny and I picked out a beautiful blue dress and braided my hair into a crown atop my head. I wanted my mother to love me and was terribly nervous about our first meeting.

After a full day of traveling, the castle finally came into view—a gigantic Gothic structure with spires that seemed to reach the sky.

Crows were lined up along the iron fence surrounding the property, and I swallowed a lump when they let out ominous caws and stared at me with their beady eyes. With each turn of the carriage wheels the ball of anxiety in my stomach grew larger.

At last, the carriage stopped in front of an imposing entrance, and I wanted nothing more than to sink into my seat and hide but I knew that would not be allowed. The daughter of a Countess did not act in such a manner. So, with my hands in my lap, I sat demurely and waited to be escorted into the house.

Borris led me into the Great Hall, where he bid me wait while he fetched Elizabeth and her husband, Ferenc, to greet me.

I craned my head back and took in the expansive ceiling. A giant chandelier was suspended high over my head with flickering candles and shimmering crystals that cast beams of light on the walls. The sight of such finery was overwhelming, and I felt certain there had been some mistake. This was the home of a princess. Not someone who grew up among farm animals and splashed through rain puddles when the nanny was not looking.

Seeing such elegance suddenly made me long for the life I left behind. However, I was determined to be a dutiful daughter and smile when my mother arrived.

A movement in the doorway caught my attention and I turned to see a woman standing there, with her hands clasped demurely in front of her. Her icy stare did nothing to quell my fears.

This was not the mother of my dreams. There was no warm embrace. No words of love. Only silent appraisal as she examined me.

The only trace of emotion was when her gaze landed on my face. Her mouth fell open just the slightest bit, and she took one step forward. Then another.

As she grew closer, the expression of disinterest was slowly replaced by disbelief. When she came within a foot of me, her hand reached out and stroked my cheek.

"You look just like him," she said with reverence.

Behind her, Ferenc walked in. His expression turned fierce as he took in our exchange.

"There is no way she will pass for my daughter," he spits out. "She looks just like her damnable father."

"Please, Ferenc," Elizabeth begged. "No one knows what he looks like."

"I know," he roared in her face. "I will not have a daily reminder that you loved another while engaged to me. Get her out of my sight."

With that, he strode out of the room and left us there.

Me, trembling. My mother, sobbing.

"Can I go back to my home?" I asked with a hopeful expression.

"Home? You are home, my dear."

"But he said…"

"Oh, that is no matter. We will just need to keep you out of sight for now." She stroked a hand down my face, and the oddest expression came over her.

"If I had known you would resemble him, I would have never let you stay away so long."

Before that day, I never knew what it meant to feel tarnished. But that sentence destroyed any illusion of normality I might have hoped for.

My mother didn't want me here to have a daughter. She wanted me here for my face. That day sealed my fate.

At first, I was allowed to stay in the nursery with a few other girls. But as the months passed, my mother's fascination with my appearance grew. So did her husband's anger.

Eventually, I was exiled to the dungeon to stay close enough to please my mother but far enough away that her husband wouldn't stumble across me.

I tried to make her love me. I tried being the dutiful daughter. But as the years passed, the futility became evident, and the light inside me dimmed. I finally realized Elizabeth only loves one person more than her dead lover. Herself.

Nothing I did or did not do would have changed my fate. Things would have unraveled the same regardless of my actions.

I push away the memories of that long-ago life. No sense in dwelling on unfortunate circumstances. I let the memories float away like leaves in the wind and bring myself back to the misery surrounding me. Tears prick my eyes but I push them back, unable to muster the energy to give into my sadness.

Hunger pains plague me throughout the night, causing me to toss and turn in my bed. The lack of food causes my limbs to grow heavy, and sleep often seems preferable over staying awake with the constant reminder of my empty stomach.

When I do manage to sleep, my dreams are unsettling. They often cause me to wake up with a gasp while I try to orient myself to my surroundings. My hunger, no doubt, is playing tricks on my mind, even in unconsciousness. The pull of my eyelids is a bittersweet release from my pain, but it only offers a momentary release before plunging me once again into the misery that surrounds me.

I roll onto my back, trying to ignore the ache which has settled deep in my bones, when a sudden noise causes me to sit upright in my bed.

Jangling keys sound from right outside my door, followed by a muffled curse. I pull the blanket up tight around my body and hold my breath, hoping that the person leaves.

The latch of my door slides open, echoing loudly in the silence, and the door is thrust open so hard it bangs against the back wall.

It is not Mother or Magda, for which I am momentarily relieved, but my relief is short-lived when Reginald steps into the room. His unkempt appearance and unshaven face look even more haggard in the moon's faint light.

He stumbles forward a few steps but catches himself before he falls to his knees. The aroma of alcohol and sweat fills the small space, and I sink back into my bed, trying unsuccessfully to distance myself from him.

He looks around the room with squinted eyes, searching for me. His eyes catch sight of me on the bed, and a devilish grin crosses his face.

"Well, well, well. What do we have here?" he asks in a slurred voice.

I stay quiet and pull the blanket closer around my body while thinking of how to avoid a confrontation with this man. He knows he is not supposed to be here. It is against my mother's orders that he converse with me, and if it is found out he saw me without my mask, he is a dead man.

“If my mother finds out you are here, death will be preferable to the pain she will inflict on you,” I say, trying to maintain a tone of superiority.

“Well, it’s a good thing she won't be finding out then, will she, Pet? Besides, I heard you aren't in her good graces at this moment, now, are you?” he sneers. “In fact, I heard that the servants are forbidden from offering you food or water until she says otherwise.”

“You will die for simply seeing me without my mask on. You know the rules.”

“Like I said, I'll only get punished if I get caught. Besides, I have this bread I thought you might like,” he said, pulling a half loaf out from beneath the lapels of his jacket. Seeing it instantly makes my mouth water, but I refrain from moving towards it.

“I wonder what a girl who hasn’t had food for three days might do for this amount of bread?” He places a finger on his chin as if contemplating his question. “I figure a kiss might get you a small slice, but for all this? We may have to come to some kind of understanding.”

“Get out of my cell, now.”

My limbs have begun to tremble, but I refuse to let the fear reflect into my voice. If animals can sense fear, I'm sure other predators can also, and this man is most certainly a predator.

"Oh, come now," he says, taking a few steps forward. "My friend Daryl and I were sitting up in the tower, sharing a pint of whiskey, and I was telling him what a waste it would be if you died down here when a person need only extend a bit of kindness to you. Kindness which might be repaid in other ways."

"Get the hell out of my room. I don't want your food. I'd rather starve than let you touch me."

Even in the low light, I can see the hard expression that crosses his face. He opens his hand and lets the loaf of bread fall to the floor with a thud.

"What a horrible waste it would be if you died down here without ever knowing a man." He takes a few steps closer to my bed and grabs his crotch, massaging himself through the fabric. "I told myself, Reggy, if that face is anything as good as her body, it would be positively sinful to let something that delectable go to waste. And I was right. You are a real beauty. Might be the prettiest I have ever seen."

My heartbeat is thundering so loudly in my ears that I can barely hear his words, but my face stays neutral while I try to think of a way out of this mess. I have no weapons in the room, and he is twice my size. The only hope I have of avoiding confrontation is using his inebriated state to my advantage and rushing around him before he has a chance to react.

"Do you know how many times I have laid in my bed with my hands in my trousers, thinking about your tight little cunt wrapped around my cock? Well, tonight, I don't have to imagine because I mean to have you."

I jump off the bed, still holding the blanket around me, and retreat until my back is firmly placed against the back wall. I stand tall as he advances towards me, even though he looks exactly like a lion about to pounce on his prey.

When he is a few feet away, I take a deep breath, gathering a wad of spit into my mouth. When he is within arm's reach, I let the spit fly directly into his face, hoping it catches him off guard. The action has the desired effect. I use his shock to my advantage and bolt past him while he rubs the saliva from his face.

A heady feeling of victory rushes through me as I sprint past him towards the open door. When I am only inches away from the threshold, my excitement comes crashing down when his fist closes around my hair, and he yanks me roughly backward into his body. I beat my fists against his large chest but he just smirks.

Starvation has weakened me and my attempts to fight him off seem pathetic. He pulls my head back by my hair and whispers in my ear.

"You think you are better than me because your mother is the Countess, but you are like every other whore I've bedded, and I'll make sure you are well and truly used before this night is through. Maybe if you ask nicely, I'll come again tomorrow night and the following one also."

He just chuckles and bites my earlobe. His sour breath invades my nostrils. If I had anything left in my stomach, I'm sure it would make a reappearance as his other hand begins to grope my breast.

A groan leaves his mouth as he rubs himself against me, and the hard outline of his erection presses painfully against my hip.

"Get the fuck off me," I say through gritted teeth before reaching down and grabbing the entire length of him and squeezing with the last bit of my last strength.

He howls in pain as I try once again to bolt forward.

Before I have even made it one step, he twirls me around and backhands me across my face so hard I sprawl across the floor in a heap. The pain from the strike is blinding. Stars explode in my vision as I lay on the ground, struggling to gather my bearings.

"You little bitch. I'll show you what real punishment looks like."

He straddles me with his massive thighs so that my body is trapped beneath him. With one swift tear, he rips open the bodice of my dress and exposes my breasts. My nipples peak when exposed to the chilly air, and he licks his lips at the sight of them.

"See? Look how your body reacts to me. I knew you were just a filthy whore like all the rest," he says before reaching down and grabbing my breasts in a savage grip.

A whimper escapes me as I squeeze my eyes shut, unable to bear the thought of his filthy hands on me.

This can't be happening. I buck against him, trying to unbalance his weight from above me, but I may as well be trying to move a mountain for all the effect it has.

If anything, my squirming seems to get him more excited, and he moves his hand from my breast to the hem of my dress.

"Oh yeah, that's what I want from you. Put up a bit of a fight. I like it when they beg."

A tear slides down my face as his hand travels up my leg, pushing my dress up and reaching for what lies beneath. When he reaches the thin barrier of fabric covering my most sensitive area, he rips it from my body with one motion.

Tears are streaming freely down my face now, and I scream.

I scream with every ounce of strength inside me until my throat is burning, and my chest feels like it might explode.

My screams echo through the cell and bounce off the walls. Reginald's laughter mixes with my screams, becoming one awful cacophony of noise.

If I could get my arms free, my fingernails would scratch at his face until he is a bloody mess, but he has them pinned under him as he continues laughing that hideous laugh. I'm sure the sound will be stuck in my head forever, and I shake my head back and forth, trying to make it stop.

When I'm certain all hope is lost, another sound emerges from the back of the cell.

A growl mingles with his laughter.

Reginald is so preoccupied with grasping at my breasts and fumbling beneath my skirt he does not notice the sound at first. It is only when the threat grows closer that his movements pause.

He turns to look at where the noise is coming from and suddenly becomes weightless. He is lifted off me with such swiftness that the air around me seems to pause while it tries to process the new development. For one moment, everything is eerily quiet.

Then the screaming starts. These screams are not like my screams, however. My screams were of terror and fear. His screams are of pain. The kind of pain that no amount of painkillers or medical intervention can help. The sound is a precursor to death.

I sit up and propel myself backward on my butt until my back hits a wall, and then I just stare. The scene unfolds, shadowed by absence of moonlight but glimpses of teeth and blood break through darkness. No matter how hard I try to look away, my gaze remains fixed on the scene unfolding in front of me.

Clashing teeth and black fur are accented by the streaks of red that now cover my cell. The screams of Reginald become weaker and farther apart until one last exhale of breath from his twitching body is all that remains of the man who is sure to haunt my future dreams.

The black wolf sits back on his haunches, breathing heavily and looking around, surveying his handy work. I should fear him after what he has done, but I don't. I feel eerily calm amid this destruction. My body begins to shake with either cold or shock. Maybe both. My head swivels from the wolf to Reginald and back to the wolf. My mind can't make sense of what just happened, nor do I want to. All that I want is to forget that this night ever happened. I want to erase it from my mind and pretend Reginald never existed.

So, I choose to do the only thing that seems like a viable option. I decide to sleep this nightmare away.

My dress hangs open where Reginald tore it, leaving me feeling exposed and vulnerable. I pull it closed and stand up. The only sound in the room is the wolf's panting and the ringing in my ears.

I am unable to process a single thought before another enters my mind. And then another. And another. My mind is a Kaleidoscope of unanswered questions, all demanding to be answered simultaneously. Squeezing my eyes shut, I push the thoughts away and drag myself over to the bed. I'm just going to sleep for a bit. The hunger and shock begin taking their toll, and I begin shaking so violently that my teeth chatter together, and my muscles quiver.

The wolf walks over to my bedside and whimpers. His hot breath washes over my face when he lays his head next to mine on the pillow. Another whimper leaves his throat and I reach out one finger, running it along his nose. He saved me, but I can't muster the energy to feel anything. Not even appreciation or thanks. I just want to sleep.

My eyelids grow heavy, and I force them open briefly when the wolf licks my hand. That one glance is all I have the energy for before drifting off into oblivion. The feeling of the wolf's body at the foot of my bed and his warm fur covering me are the last things I feel before falling asleep.

Chapter 5.

I wake up the next day feeling surprisingly well-rested. The place at the foot of my bed is still warm from where the wolf must have recently departed. The heat from his body helped remove the chill from my bones, and I stretch my arms high over my head to remove the last vestiges of sleep before surveying the destruction of the room.

Streaks of blood cover a good portion of the floor, with some splattering onto the walls where the wolf must have delivered the deadly blow. Reginald's body is hunched over against the wall across from me. There is no denying that the man is dead. His mouth is open wide in a silent scream, and the vacant look on his face is obvious that his soul has left his body.

If the bastard had a soul, to begin with.

I am having a hard time feeling even an ounce of sorrow for this man who terrorized me only hours ago. The best I can do is pity, and even that is a stretch.

Swinging my legs over the bed, I spot the loaf of bread Reginald brought with him last night, which, surprisingly, does not have a speck of blood on it. Despite the carnage around me, I am ravenously hungry and take a bite of the loaf. My throat feels raw from screaming last night, as well as dry from lack of water. The snow stopped falling yesterday, and I haven't had anything to quench my throat in nearly an entire day.

Turning in circles, I go over my options on how to proceed. The cell door is open, thanks to Reginald, and all I need to do to be free is step over the threshold. The thought both terrifies and thrills me. This has never been an option for me, and the thought makes me lightheaded.

I have very limited knowledge of the outside world and have no idea how to survive outside these walls, but anything is preferable to staying here another moment. With that in mind, I tuck the rest of the bread away in the pocket of my dress and begin preparing for my journey into the woods.

Reginald's boots are too big for me, but with enough padding, they will do the trick until I find something more suitable. I remove his jacket from his body, which is rather tricky since his limbs are stiff with death.

The fabric stinks of him, and I want to toss it back on the ground, but it is nearly winter and I need to keep out the bite of the cold wind. So, I swallow down my revulsion and drape it across my shoulders. I comfort myself that once we are outside, the smell will diminish.

I hope.

Ripping strips from my blanket, I tie cloth around my hands and wrap the rest of the blanket around my shoulders like a cape. This will have to do.

I'm a sorry sight with my too-big shoes and makeshift winterwear, but the last thing I am worried about is my appearance.

My first few steps outside my cell are tentative. I expect someone to shout down the corridor and notify the castle of my escape, but all stays silent. When at last, the entrance of the dungeon is directly in front of me, I step out and take a deep breath.

The winter air filters in through my lungs, and I take another step and then another. My head swivels from side to side, but the trees are still, and all is quiet. No one is watching or waiting for me. No one is going to stop me.

My steps grow faster with each passing second until I am running full speed towards the tree line. I don't know how to process all of my emotions, so instead, I shut them down and focus on moving towards the trees and away from the clutches of my mother. The oversized boots are awkward, and I trip more than once, but never slow. I just pick myself up and keep going.

Once a few minutes pass, and I put a fair amount of distance between the castle and myself, I fall to my knees and try to control my breathing. Placing a hand on the tree next to me, I lean my head against it until my heartbeat slows and my breath comes out in white puffs.

Then I begin to laugh. I laugh until my side hurts, and tears run from my eyes. This is the moment I have dreamed of for so long, and it is finally here. Finally, my laughter subsides and I wipe the tears from my eyes before standing up and begin my journey again.

I decide to travel down the mountain and towards the road. A road must lead to a town, so I begin my journey onward.

A crunch of leaves behind me causes my head to swivel, but whatever is outside my field of vision lets out an angry snarl. I hold my breath to see if it will make an appearance, and let out a relieved breath when the crunching of leaves indicates it is moving away from me.

Many woodland animals come and go through this forest, but other creatures also frequent these mountains—hideous, mutated creatures. I have seen them on more than one occasion, and every time they appear, the sight of them leaves me trembling. They are not quite man and not quite animal. They stand on two legs but have grotesque features, twisted into something resembling a nightmare. Some have horns. Others have hooves. They are all different but equally terrifying.

I quicken my steps, hoping whatever is behind me doesn't change its mind and return. Every few feet, I turn around to check on my progress and make sure nothing is following me.

It does not take me long to realize I am being followed. Out of the corner of my eye, I catch sight of black fur darting behind bushes.

Although he is trying to avoid being detected, the wolf's dark fur stands out in contrast to the patches of snow, and I nearly laugh at his attempts to remain hidden. Another glance back shows his head peeking out from behind a bush. He quickly retreats when he catches my gaze.

It seems like he wants to play hide and seek but only to be the hider.

We go on like this for some time. Eventually, we give up on the charade, and he walks next to me as we make our way down the incline.

I take small bites of the bread in my pocket and scoop up snow from the ground to rinse it down with. It occurs to me that this bread won't last long, and I should try to find an alternate source of sustenance.

The forest must be full of food, and I begin to keep an eye out for anything that looks like it might be edible. I have very little knowledge about this sort of thing, but have seen servants go into the forest to gather mushrooms and roots. Surely, there must be an abundance of food to be found here.

The forest floor is littered with leaves where the foliage is too dense for snow to accumulate, and I brush my feet along the path, trying to uncover something to eat.

We walk this way for several hours, and I have nearly given up hope of finding anything when I uncover several mushrooms hidden under a patch of leaves. Smiling, I point them out to the wolf, who tilts his head sideways and perks up his ears.

I grab one of the mushrooms and pop it into my mouth.

The cook at the castle occasionally adds mushrooms to my watery soups, but nothing prepares me for the bitter flavor of this one. Beggars can't be choosers however, so I force myself to swallow it and shudder in disgust.

The wolf lets out a yip and begins circling the patch of remaining mushrooms. I attempt to shoo him away before reaching down for another one. He lets out another loud bark before lifting his leg and urinating all over them.

"Hey! What did you do that for?" I ask indignantly.

He lets out another bark before circling me in an agitated state.

Huffing out a breath, I start moving down the hill again, still angry about the soiled mushrooms behind me. That was enough food to nearly fill my belly, and now I'll have to continue walking just as hungry as I was before.

I perk up when a bush with bright red berries nestled among the green sprigs of leaves comes into view.

Excellent, I think, reaching for a juicy-looking bunch. I frown in confusion as my hand passes through the cluster of berries, not touching them. What in the world? I try again but have the same luck as last time. Holding my hand up, I wave it in front of my face. The movement seems too slow, as if it is someone else's hand, and I have no control over its speed.

"What is happening?" I say in a thick voice.

I turn around in confusion as my voice echoes behind me and into the trees. It resounds repeatedly until I hold my hands up to my ears to keep the echo out.

Trying to take a step, I only succeed in stumbling and falling to the ground, where I remain, trying to figure out what in the world is happening.

The wolf barks again, and he runs in frantic circles around me. He pulls at my blanket with his teeth, trying to rouse me from the ground with limited success. His body becomes one long blur of black fur, and I reach out to touch it, but my hand misses its mark and ends up in a cold pile of mud instead. He stands before me, and I focus on the browns of his eyes. So beautiful. The flecks of brown seem to move together in waves before bouncing out of his eyes and morphing into the sky to mingle with the clouds.

I fall back onto the ground and stare at the sky, letting the brown clouds dance in front of my eyes like frolicking children, laughing and dancing to an unknown beat. Laughter bubbles inside my chest as I watch them, wanting to join them in their merriment.

Next, I am floating in the sky. I fling my arms wide, ready to embrace my imminent arrival of the clouds.

I am lifted higher and notice, in some distant part of my brain, that warm arms embrace me. Warm amber eyes float above me as I am carried through the trees. I could happily live in this world of suspended animation forever if given the chance. Why has no one ever brought me here before? It is quite a wonderful place to be.

All at once, the happy, frolicking children in the sky turn into wild beasts with gnashing teeth and razor-sharp claws. They begin howling angrily and swooping down from their perches in the sky. I thrash at them, fighting them off with all my might, but strong arms hold my arms to my side, and a comforting voice whispers in my ear. My heart is beating so fiercely that I can hear every beat in my head. It sounds like someone is beating a drum beat with the steady thrum, thrum, thrum of a massive mallet, and I throw my hands over my ears to make it stop.

"Come now, Little Bird. Drink this. It will make you feel better."

I listen to the voice and drink. I need something, anything, to make this nightmare go away. I drink greedily until the cup is empty, and lick the rim to catch any last droplets.

Then the pain comes. A ripple of agony shoots across my stomach, so intense it causes me to double over and gasp for breath. The pain continues, coming wave after wave until I mercifully vomit up the contents of my stomach.

Only once everything has evacuated my body does the pain relent.

I lay there, shaking and sweating profusely under my clothing. The blanket around me suddenly feels too hot, and I kick my legs to try to remove it, but I am held down by strong hands that refuse to let me go.

"Hot. Hot, hot," I repeat, unable to handle the heat scorching under the surface of my skin.

"You need to sweat the rest of the poison out of you," I hear the voice say from a distant place.

Then I begin to cry. I can't control the well of emotion that suddenly bursts forth from me. The last few days have all been too much. One person can only handle so much torment, and this pain is the icing on the top of the cake. I break down into sobs and grasp the arm that is holding me down. I need a small measure of support, and if hanging onto a stranger's arm brings me that comfort, then so be it.

"Shh now, Little Bird."

A hand begins stroking the hair back from my face, and cool lips touch my forehead. "All will be well soon. Just sleep for now. It will be better when you wake up. I promise."

And so, I do. I fall into a deep, tormented sleep full of wild, angry beasts and things that move in an impossibly fluid way. My eyelids fight to open, but every time I try to pull myself out of unconsciousness, I am sucked back down into the depths of my dreams.

Finally, after what seems like an eternity, consciousness begins to seep into the edges of my foggy brain.

No screams. No snarling beasts. No dungeon.

I inhale deeply, savoring the moment before reality seeps in and ruins it. A smell invades my nose when I pull in a deep breath.

The smell of wood smoke and fur. Winter nights and raw meat. Pine needles and hickory. All the scents mingle together and confuse my senses. They seem to blend perfectly but don't belong together at all.

I wonder briefly if perhaps I am dead.

No. If I were dead, there would be no pain. My aching head and stomach assure me that I am, in fact, alive.

Cool liquid is poured onto my lips, and I drink it up eagerly, letting it soothe my chapped lips. The cool fluid feels good against my throat, and a moan escapes me. I try turning my head to see who is holding the glass, but a searing pain flashes across my head.

"Slowly now," the voice said. "You mustn't rush it. Normally, the mushroom would have had much milder effects, but with your empty stomach and slight frame, the effect was much more potent."

Turning slowly, I open my eyes just a fraction to see a man sitting beside me. The first thing about him that draws my attention is his eyes. They are a deep amber, and his eyebrows are tipped up in concern.

His brown hair is pulled back into a ponytail at the base of his neck, but several strands are loose and hang around his face. He has not shaved recently, and a thick stubble is growing on his face, making it look darker and more dangerous than his age should allow.

He can't be much older than me. Perhaps in his mid-twenties, if I am being generous. And here he is, catering to some half-starved girl who was silly enough to eat a poisoned mushroom.

"How.... How did I get here?" I croak out. My voice is still raw from thirst.

"I found you in the woods, not far from here. Luckily, I heard the wolf howling, and got that tea into you in time, or you may not have survived the poison."

"Where is the wolf now? He... He saved me." The image of him urinating on the rest of the mushrooms returns with sudden clarity, and now I realize why. He must have known. Somehow, he knew.

"Oh, he comes and goes as he pleases. Don't worry about that now. You just focus on resting."

He smooths back a piece of hair that has fallen across my brow. "I'll start some broth on the stove and see if your stomach will allow you to eat a little something."

He stands off the bed, and the air around me is immediately colder without him there. I reach out to call him back, but know that is silly and let my arm fall back to my side.

While he is stoking the fire and gathering ingredients for the broth, I inspect the surroundings.

The entire house is one large room. The interior is sparse but clean, with minimal furnishings. A roaring fireplace is on the opposite wall from where I lie in a small but comfortable bed. Drying herbs hang from the rafters, and an earthy scent of rosemary and thyme is thick in the air. The furnishings may be sparse, but his affection for books is evident since most of the available wall space is filled with shelves to store them.

I am envious of this wealth of knowledge that is readily available to him. I have not had any books at my disposal for years. My mother said the knowledge would be wasted on me. Now I know why she said that, although it did not make sense at the time. My thoughts wander back to my last encounter with her, but I brush away the memory and focus again on my surroundings.

The man leaves the house before returning with an armful of firewood. The scent of freshly cut wood fills the room, and I breathe deeply, memorizing the heady aroma. He dumps the wood near the fireplace and stacks it in a pile. His entire demeanor looks so perfectly composed and confident that it appears as if he has never seen a day of hardship in his whole life.

I turn onto my side so we are facing each other. “What is your name?” I ask in a hoarse voice, not wanting to continue thinking of him as, the man.

“Rowan,” he replies, still stacking the logs. “And you would be?”

“Anastasia.”

“That doesn’t suit you. I prefer Little Bird,” he replies, turning around to look at me with a smirk.

His lopsided grin causes my heartbeat to quicken, and I feel my face flush with heat. I don't tell him that it is presumptuous of him to give me a nickname after we just met. Secretly, I am thrilled by his words. No one has ever given me a nickname, and I quite like it.

A pot of broth is soon simmering over the fireplace, and he uses a ladle to fill a ceramic mug with the most delicious thing I have ever smelled.

I prop myself up in bed, and he hands me the steaming mug before returning to the stove to get one for himself.

My stomach screams at me to devour it as fast as possible, but I sip it slowly, not wanting to make myself sick. Tendrils of steam rise from the frothy liquid and I put the mug under my nose to enjoy the rich smell before taking my first sip. It is salty and delicious, with bits of meat and vegetables swirling just below the surface.

Rowan sits at the foot of the bed and leans back against the wall, closing his eyes and sighing contentedly. He occasionally takes sips of his steaming cup but remains silent while I study him.

I struggle with what questions to ask him. This is my first time interacting with anyone besides my mother in so long I forgot how to act around other people.

I finally decide, since he seems content to sit in silence and enjoy his drink, I will do the same.

A smile tugs at the corners of my mouth as I process my predicament.

Yes. It was a hellish beginning to my freedom, but the reality of being out in the world hits me square in the chest. I am truly free. A shiver of excitement snakes down my spine. For the first time since I was ten years old, I feel like I can breathe again.

My mother won't be happy once she discovers I am gone, but that is a worry for another day. I have learned to enjoy life's small pleasures, no matter how fleeting they may be. Tonight, with a blazing fireplace and a delicious cup of broth, I will count myself blessed.

When I take another sip of broth, my smile grows wider, and a small bubble of sound escapes my lips. The sound is so foreign to me that I almost don't recognize it for what it is.

Laughter.

Rowan opens one eye and smiles at me before returning to his place of rest against the wall. He seems to be a man of few words, not needing to fill the silence with useless chatter. I like that about him. I have been in silence for so long that too much conversation would be overwhelming.

Few men resided at the castle during my time there, but the ones I have encountered are either dirty guards with appalling manners or pompous royalty.

Rowan seems to be neither of those. He is dressed in a simple shirt and trousers with nothing covering his feet. A leather belt hangs around his waist, which appears to be more for practical purposes than for fashion.

Something makes me want to wind myself around this man and never let go. He has a warmth about this that makes it feel like everything will be okay. After everything I have been through lately, it is precisely what I need right now.

I take a few more moments studying him while his eyes are closed, absorbing every detail of his profile. He has a long, lean frame and a sun-kissed face. The fingers wrapped around the mug are long and unblemished, but his arms have thick cords of muscles running through them. He is obviously used to hard work, but doesn't have the bone-weary look of defeat that many laborers possess. No. He looks to be thriving on manual labor rather than suffering from it.

Heat begins to crawl up my neck when I let my gaze travel down his legs and back up to his torso, stopping for a fraction of a second on the bulge between his thighs.

"Do you like what you see?" he asks. His eyes are still closed and there is a hint of laughter in his voice.

I choke on a sip of broth and use my coughing episode as an excuse not to answer.

His eyes were closed. How in the world did he know I was studying him?

My cheeks are flaming hot, and I try to think of anything else to keep my mind off this man's beautiful body. I don't know what my problem is. Suddenly, the thought of his warm hands on me consumes my thoughts. I clear my throat, trying to sound unaffected by his presence.

"Where are we exactly?"

"Just sleep now, Little Bird. We have plenty of time for questions tomorrow. For now, you need rest so your body can heal."

But I have so many questions to ask. Does he know where I can go after recovering?

Where are we now? Will he allow me to stay a few days? Or will he force me to leave as soon as I wake? I have so many things I need to know, but I can already feel the weight of sleep tugging at me. He is right. My body needs to rest, and I can wait a few more hours to ask him questions.

My empty cup of broth is pulled away as my eyes flutter closed, and I sink back down to lay my head on the pillow. His fingers brush against my cheek as he pulls the blanket up around my shoulders and tucks it around me. I have never had someone take care of me with such tenderness. A sense of loss hits me when he stands up from the bed, and I immediately miss his warmth as he walks to the other side of the room.

He places the two empty mugs down and lies next to the fireplace.

I force my eyes to stay open for a few more moments, taking in the way the firelight plays across his face. It is that image I have burned into the back of my eyelids as sleep claims me once again.

Chapter 6.

My first thought upon waking up is that I must still be dreaming. Sunshine streams through the window, and a fresh gust of air blows through the room. Wiping the sleep from my eyes, I hear laughter coming from somewhere in the distance. It sounds like children's laughter, full of excitement and energy, just bursting to explore the wide world of their imagination.

Okay, now I know I must be dreaming.

I haven't seen another child for... well since I was a child myself. The laughter transports me to a time when I still retained my childish innocence. Back to a time when I still believed in happy endings.

Before being thrown into the dungeon like a common criminal, I was allowed to stay in the nursery of the castle, just so long as I stayed out of sight. Four other children were there with me, all lined up like little dolls to be gazed upon and pampered but never to be heard.

We were taught how to behave like royalty and exhibit proper etiquette. The other children were girls, like me, but instead of being born into nobility, they were the children of lower-class peasants.

They were given to my mother to pay off debts which they incurred from not being able to pay taxes on their farmland. It was a brutal method of guaranteeing she got whatever was owed to her, but it ensured that no one would doubt her repercussions if the debt remained unpaid. My mother did not make idle threats. If you had a child, she would take it as repayment. If you did not have a child, she would take a limb or worse. Your life.

During my childhood, it was a blessing to have these other girls to play with. They were like sisters to me for a brief period, and I can still see their smiling faces as we ran around the room, singing nursery rhythms and playing with our wooden dolls. This time was precious to me, and I often wonder what happened to those girls after I was taken.

Did they grow up to become wives and mothers? Were they married off to wealthy aristocracy around the country? Or did something sinister happen to them? Did my mother get sick of them and dispose of them to fill her sick appetite? Perhaps they became indentured servants, still repaying their family's debt.

Whatever their fate, I pray it turned out well for them. Or if not well, at least that their ending was swift.

However, now, I shake off the memory and inch closer to the window to see if I can find out where this laughter is coming from. Before I could peek over the ledge, the window frame swings open and three blonde children pop their heads up, peering in through the window.

I shoot backward, startled at the sudden appearance. Before I can catch myself, I fall onto my backside with a thump. Pain shoots up my tailbone, and I let out a startled cry. The children's eyes widen, and they quickly scramble away from the window.

At that moment, Rowan comes in through the front door carrying a bucket of fresh water.

"Did you see them?" I ask, pointing towards the window.

"Who?"

"The children. There were three of them, and they had blonde curly hair."

He looks out the window and chuckles. "You must have scared them half to death. They are running like a Wyvern is fresh on their tails."

"A Wyvern?"

"Yes. A fierce, fire-breathing dragon with a barbed tail and laser eyes," he replies, as if it were obvious.

My own eyes grow wide at the description.

“It is only a fairy tale,” he says when he sees my startled reaction. “They were likely just shocked at seeing a lady in my house. They usually pop their head through my window every morning to see if I have a trinket for them from my travels.”

“Why don’t they use your door?”

“It's become something of a tradition that started when they were only babes on their mothers' hips. My sister, Lynet, would come and say good morning to me every day through this window. It seemed to catch on, and now my window is used more often than my door,” he chuckles.

“Your sister? So that would mean they are your nephews?”

“That's right. I'm the proud uncle of those three and many more. My sisters seem to have a penchant for staying pregnant,” he chuckles.

His lopsided grin does funny things to my stomach, and I swallow a surge of emotion as he helps me up from my place on the floor. Rubbing my hand over my backside, I attempt to soothe the ache caused by the fall.

“I got some fresh water,” Rowan said, placing it on a hook near the fireplace. It will be warm in no time, and you can use it to wash the dirt from your body if you like. I will leave you to get freshened up and be back in a half hour or so with some fresh bread and cheese."

My stomach rumbles at the thought of food, and I realize I am ravenous with hunger.

"Thank you. That is very kind of you."

"You may want to err... ...close the blinds before you wash, in case I get any more visitors," he says with a wink.

A blush creeps up my face, and I turn away before he can see it.

"Lynet gave me an extra dress for you also. I put it on the chair if you would like something fresh to change into."

"Oh, I couldn't possibly take her dress."

"It's no problem. She is happy to help."

I look down at my dress and groan. Not only is the front of it tied together in an attempt to provide me with a bit of dignity, but it is covered in filth from my illness. Sweat stains are evident across my torso, and vomit is speckled across the hem of my dress.

"Perhaps I will take it. Please tell her I am very grateful for her kindness."

My embarrassment at accepting her dress is not nearly as bad as my revulsion at being in this sorry state. I will be sure to do something nice for her in return for her kindness.

"You can tell her yourself if you like. I thought we could take a walk later and meet a few people. The fresh air will do you good."

Anxiety threatens to claw up my chest at all the unknowns.

Are they nice? Will they like me? Will they judge me for spending the night in a man's house? And where exactly is here? Where in the world am I?

Instead of releasing a barrage of questions, I settle on just one.

"Where exactly are we?"

"This is Coillte Domhain."

"Wait," I say, too loudly, as he opens the door to leave. "What does that mean?"

"Welcome to the Dark Woods, Little Bird," he says with a devilish grin. And just like that, he's gone.

"The Dark Woods? What in the world is that supposed to mean?" I huff in exasperation.

More and more questions keep circling in my brain, but I push them away while I prepare to wash. *One thing at a time. Just focus on the present and all it has to offer.*

Peeling my dress off, I cringe when I notice the exact state of my body. Ugh, dirt covers nearly every inch of my skin, and the smell coming from me is nearly enough to make my eyes water.

Just perfect.

The first man I meet in nearly a decade who doesn't try to assault me, and it smells as if

I have been wallowing in the mud with the swine.

Well, what's done is done, and there is no use dwelling on it.

Instead, I begin the methodical process of wiping my skin clean and wrapping my hair in something resembling order. I give up trying to smooth out the snarls and settle on a loose braid that falls to the middle of my back. Next, I put on the new dress, reveling in the soft fabric against my bare skin and the fresh scent of pine and honey that clings to it.

There are no undergarments to put on underneath since both my chemise and underwear were torn by Reginald during his assault.

At first, the lack of proper garments leaves me feeling exposed and I think of how to remedy the situation. I am certainly not going to ask Lynet for her undergarment.

I soon realize it isn't so bad. I actually quite enjoy the added bit of freedom. However, a light breeze will surely make its way under my dress and chill the sensitive area between my thighs.

The dress is a tad long for me, but otherwise, it is nearly a perfect fit, and I thank my lucky stars that Rowan's sister and I are so close in size.

Sitting on the bed, I wait for Rowan to return with the bread and cheese but quickly decide against sitting still. I walk around the room, fingering the objects and smelling the aromatic herbs. When he finally enters a short time later, I have my nose buried deep inside a bunch of lavender, smelling its sweet fragrance.

"You like Lavender?" he asks, closing the door behind him.

"Oh yes. I haven't smelled it since I was a child, but it is one of my favorite memories. Running through a lavender field with my arms outstretched to the sky. Nothing compares to that kind of childish freedom." I smile sadly.

"You would be surprised."

"How so?"

"Sit, and I will show you." He grins wickedly before pulling something out of the basket, slung over his arm. "Now close your eyes."

A nervous laugh escapes my throat before I sit on the bed and close my eyes.

For a split second, I wonder if this is all some elaborate joke and if I am simply a fool for going along with it. A moment later, that thought leaves my mind completely.

This scent of a rich, meaty stew envelops me, and my stomach grumbles in anticipation. Most of my meals at the castle were watery soups made with potatoes or various other vegetables.

The scent grows stronger, and I must force myself to keep my eyes closed even as the lids flicker in defiance.

Something is pushed to my lips, and I automatically open my mouth, needing to taste whatever has created such an appetizing aroma.

My eyes fly open as the flavor of the stew explodes on my tongue.

The mixture of herbs and tender meat is almost too much to bear, and an embarrassingly loud moan escapes my throat moments before my eyes drift closed once again. I savor the stew for a few moments longer before resignedly swallowing, already missing the incredible taste.

"I hope you remember this moment as fondly as you do the lavender field," Rowan says, handing me the rest of the stew.

"Aren't you having any?" I ask.

"I ate at Lynet's house already with her and the children. She sent along the stew as an apology for not having the cheese I promised you."

"Oh, Rowan. I have never tasted anything so delicious," I say through another spoonful. Remembering my manners, I swallow my next bite before speaking again. "Where in the world did she learn to cook like this?"

"My mother was a wonderful cook, as was her mother and her mother before her."

"Where is your mother now?"

I regret the question the moment the words leave my mouth. His eyes turn from a warm brown to an icy black in one instant. His usually cheery disposition becomes a hard, impenetrable barrier.

The food suddenly feels like a rock in my stomach, and I tense, waiting for what he will say next.

Rowan shakes his head and closes his eyes. The muscles in his jaws flex. Open and closed. Open and closed. His internal struggle is obvious, and I sink back into the bed while I wait for the wave of emotion to pass.

When he opens his eyes again, the old Rowan is back.

"She hasn't been here for a long time now. She left when I was young, and Lynet raised me and my other siblings."

"Other siblings? How many do you have?"

"I have four older sisters. All of which I am thankful for every day."

My body relaxes again, and I wisely decide to hold back further questioning about his mother. I eat the rest of the food in silence before leaning back on the bed and patting my stomach.

"Ugh, I think I may have eaten too much."

"I do the same every time I eat her cooking. It's a miracle I don't weigh as much as a horse with all the baked goods and sweets she pushes on me."

He takes the bowl from me and stands to wash it in the water bucket, but he changes his mind once he sees the filthy water.

"I don't think I have ever seen water that shade of brown before," he jokes. "But I must say you do appear much cleaner."

I blush and look down to hide my embarrassment. "Yes, I don't think I have ever been that filthy in my life."

"Well, my nose thanks you for the improvement, madam."

"Hey!" I say in mock outrage. "I couldn't help it. I was sick."

As I try to hide my amusement and feign anger, laughter bubbles up and slips over before I can control it.

"I did have a rather particular smell, didn't I?"

"I am not one to judge. I have had my bouts of sickness that would put yours to shame. I nearly died when I was eight from a prolonged sickness."

"Really? That sounds horrible."

"Oh, it was. The fever consumed me for six days and nights before it finally broke. Lynet had to wash the bedding several times a day. I got sick all over everything, and the blankets were soaked with sweat. I don't remember much of it, but I do remember the nightmares were horrible. Ghastly dreams of monsters and demons coming to steal my soul and drag me straight down into the murky depths with them."

"To hell?"

"Hell, the Abyss, the Netherlands. Whatever it was, I don't want to be there."

"Do you believe in hell?" I ask, genuinely interested.

"I believe life continues after we are dead. Whatever form that takes is up to you. I prefer to think of the earth absorbing my body and soul and that I will re-emerge as something else. Maybe a tree or a bird. Anything that is alive and makes me feel free."

"That sounds wonderful. A much more peaceful prospect than the fire and brimstones I was taught as a little girl."

While my mother often indulges in many forbidden desires behind closed doors, to the public eye, she is a devout catholic woman and presents herself as such in public.

Early on, it was drilled into me that I should do God's bidding or suffer the consequences. However, those warnings have faded with time and now seem more like a fairy tale than facts.

"Is that what you believe happens when you die?" he asks with a quirk of his head.

"I don't know what I believe in. Maybe nothing."

It feels like such a letdown after his impassioned speech, but my soul feels empty. I don't feel a calling to a greater being nor the passion he boasts about so freely. I only feel alone. It is all I have ever felt. Or at least, that is all I have felt since arriving at Castle Cachtice.

"We all believe in something. Sometimes it just takes us longer to figure out what that something is." He winks. "Now, how about that walk? The weather is incredibly warm for a late fall day. We should indulge ourselves before the real frost sets in. Besides, some fresh air might be just the thing to get rid of the rest of that smell."

I smack him with the back of my hand. "You are positively infuriating." But I laugh despite myself.

He has a way of lightening any mood, which I like. It seems he can turn any subject into something enjoyable and lighthearted.

Any subject except his mother.

Chapter 7.

We step outside into the fresh air, which is cool but not uncomfortably so. It feels good to let the chilled air into my lungs, and I breathe deeply, letting the freshness penetrate my lungs.

A few leaves still stubbornly cling to the tree branches, refusing to give in to their inevitable downfall. The nearly empty branches allow rays of sunshine to filter through, forcing me to squint as my eyes adjust to the brightness. Warmth soaks into my skin as I am swathed in a spot of sunshine, and I tilt my face to the sky with a smile. What I see above me is nothing short of amazing.

I must look like a fool. My mouth is wide open, and I stare, unblinking, at the sight before me.

Nearly every house in the village is built into the trees. Giant oaks cradle the structures between their mighty limbs like outstretched hands.

Each tree has a ladder affixed to the front so the villagers can easily ascend to their dwellings. Long bridges made of vines and wooden treads zigzag between the houses to connect the entire town above the ground.

It seems like something out of a fairy tale book.

Some houses appear ancient, with vines climbing up the sides and weathered wood siding. Others seem like they have been recently built with fresh tan wood and gleaming windows. Their thatched roofs are well-tended, and most are surrounded by porches with railings for the inhabitants to sit outside and enjoy the ambiance of this magnificent forest.

Rowan's house is simpler than most of the other houses, and I wonder why he chose to live on the ground instead of one of those magnificent dwellings.

I can't see the entire village from this vantage point, but I already count at least two dozen houses. My head swivels from side to side as I take it all in, but reality refuses to take root inside my brain.

I have never seen anything so magnificent.

"How many people live here?" I finally manage to squeak out.

"In all, we have nearly one hundred residents."

My attention snaps to a set of children running across one of the bridges, causing it to sway as they run along the swinging expanse.

They don't seem bothered in the slightest as it rocks beneath them.

One of the children stops to lean over the side of the bridge and waves down at us.

"Rowan! Up here," the child yells.

"Hello, Ewin!" Rowan replies. "We will be up in a moment."

"Up?" I ask, suddenly terrified.

I don't have a fear of heights exactly, but the thought of walking across those swinging precipices suddenly terrifies me.

Rowan squeezes my waist with one hand, and his touch is enough to snap me out of my wide-eyed shock. Even through the fabric of my dress, I can feel the warmth of his hand. I force myself not to lean into him, demanding more.

"You will be fine. I promise you," he says, squeezing once more before turning towards the tree.

With that, we walk to a ladder at the base of a nearby tree and begin to ascend.

As I climb the wooden planks, a breeze sweeps the hair off the back of my neck. My heart beats a bit faster with each rung until I'm sure my heart will beat right out of my chest. Breathe. Just breathe. And don't look down.

Of course, I look down.

My fingernails dig into the current rung, and I bite down the fear that threatens to choke me.

Closing my eyes, I count to ten. The familiar repetition helps stop my limbs from trembling, and I climb again.

On the last rung, Rowan pulls me onto a landing platform.

With my heart beating wildly in my chest, I walk off the central platform and onto the bridge. With each step, the wood groans beneath my feet, and I hold my breath, expecting the entire thing to come crashing down. I mentally calculate the probability of surviving the fall but decide the odds are not in my favor.

I peel my gaze away from the precarious drop and focus on what's before me.

It's Rowan's backside.

Well, at least it's a better distraction than thinking about how long I might survive with two broken legs.

I smirk as his swaying hips accentuate the rather nice asset beneath his trousers. It seems to be the perfect distraction, and my heart begins to slow.

The bridge is much sturdier than it appears from the ground, and I breathe easier the further we go. That is until a little ball of energy with blonde hair runs towards us from the other end, sending the entire bridge swaying violently.

I clutch the railing and squeeze my eyes shut tight as the ground beneath my feet continues to sway back and forth. When the shaking finally subsides, I look down to see a boy of perhaps six or seven staring up at me expectantly.

"Hello," the child says. "My name is Ewin."

"Hello, Ewin," I respond, releasing my death grip on the railing and shaking his offered hand. "I'm Anastasia."

"That's a funny name," he says, screwing up his face and looking to his uncle for confirmation.

"Ewin," Rowan says in a low voice.

"Well, it is," the child replies with exasperation. "Can I call you Anya instead? I like that better."

"Ewin!" Rowan warns again.

"No, that's okay. I like the name Anya better also," I reply with a wink towards Ewin.

"I like her," he says with a smile that shows off a missing front tooth and a set of dimples that will cause women to swoon over him when he is older.

Without warning, he sprints off in the other direction and sends the bridge swinging again.

Before I can catch myself, my body pitches forward straight into Rowan's hard chest. I grasp his waist tightly to keep from falling over.

"I will remember that bringing you up here is all it takes to get your hands on me."

This man is insufferable.

"Just so you know. I had no intention of putting my hands all over you, as you so delicately put it," I reply indignantly.

Although, if I must admit, taking my hands off him is harder than it should be, even as I huff in mock anger.

"Liar." He smirks before turning and continuing our trek along the bridge.

I don't answer because I'm sure he can tell I am lying by how my face flushes when he looks at me. Or even worse, when I am looking at him.

It isn't my fault he has such an appealing physique. Maybe if I pretend he has a wart on his nose, it will be enough to deter my wayward thoughts.

I focus all my energy on conjuring up such thoughts, and when he looks back at me, I imagine he has a giant oozing wart right on the end of his nose. But when his eyes twinkle, and he gives me that lopsided grin, poof, the wart is gone, and my thighs are wet.

Damn, my wayward thoughts.

Luckily, I am saved from any further provocative images of his backside when we come to a large platform set directly in the middle of the elevated town. From this vantage point, I can see the entire village and turn in circles to survey the buildings.

Rowan leans on the railing and points out an elderly couple. They are playing a game of chess together outside their home in weathered wooden chairs. The elderly man has his fist placed under his chin with a solemn look of concentration while the woman sits back, looking as smug as a cat with a bowl of cream.

"Those are the founders of this town. The woman's name is Fern, and the man is her husband, Gordon. They formed this town seventy years ago when they were both just teenagers. They fled into the woods to escape persecution for their faith and brought several like-minded individuals with them. Since then, the town has grown to what you see here today. It is a collection of people who practice whatever faith they wish, whatever way they wish to practice it. There is no government to inflict taxes and no society to condemn actions. They ask only that everyone remain peaceful and open-minded."

"So, they rule this town?"

"No. There are no rulers. There is no one to say what we must do or how it must be done. Everyone does their part, and we lean on each other when community is needed."

"But what happens when someone doesn't contribute or becomes a nuisance?"

"It is rare, but a few times, people have been banished from our town. Whether they took advantage or inflicted harm on others, it is not tolerated. It is not a rule, but we can ban together collectively and vote to remove others from our midst if the majority is in favor."

"Who can come here? I mean, is it open to anyone that wishes to join?" I ask, leaning against the railing and enjoying his easy company.

"Generally, yes. We have never turned anyone away. However, whether they wish to stay on long or short-term is up to them. Sometimes, people leave after a few short weeks. Others spend their lives here, even if the offerings are limited."

"Why would they leave? It seems so idyllic here."

"We are far away from any town or city. Luxuries which are available to others are not available to us. We occasionally leave to trade with merchants, but for the most part, we fend for ourselves."

"It seems like a small price to pay for such serenity."

"Also, some people leave for a short period to find a companion. The pool of possible candidates would get small very quickly if we didn't look for someone outside this village, we weren't related to," he says with a grin.

"Have you?" I ask, suddenly feeling shy. "Have you looked for someone outside this village?"

He leans back on the railing and peers at me with an unnerving intensity.

"There is no one out there I am interested in."

The air suddenly becomes difficult to breathe with him staring at me like that, and I clear my throat before changing the subject.

"What about food? You can grow enough to feed all these people?" I ask.

"We hunt and gather, but a large amount of our food does come from the community garden as well as our private gardens."

People walk along paths beneath us, carrying baskets and bags full of fresh bread. They stop to talk and laugh while going about their daily chores. The contentment on their faces is evident, and I am a bit jealous of their day-to-day roles among the trees.

Even a pregnant lady with a considerable round bump and a toddler trailing behind her is hefting a laundry basket down the street. But she doesn't look dejected or overworked like the servants in my mother's castle did. No. She is glowing. When she crosses paths with a young man, he offers to take the basket for her and carries it up a ladder to her house. Everything seems to fit perfectly in its place here among the trees, and I sigh with contentment.

Closing my eyes, I step forward and press myself against the railing. Wood smoke from a nearby stove tinges the air with a rustic quality, and I breathe deeply to capture the smell before it is blown away. A light breeze lifts my hair and blows it around me, causing the strands to tickle my face. I throw my arms out wide and soak in the moment of freedom.

"Do you think this is what it feels like to fly?" I ask.

When Rowan doesn't answer, I crack open one eye and take in his amused expression. "What? You never wondered what it would feel like to soar through the trees?"

"I haven't given it much thought," he replies.

I sigh. "I have. I have thought about it for the past eight years, and this comes pretty close to what I imagined it would be like."

"You deserve to fly, Little Bird."

The look of sincerity on his face makes me want to weep, and I brush away an unshed tear from my eye. This is everything I ever dreamed of. A niggling worry snakes into the back of my mind, telling me that it is too good to be true. Too good to last forever. The thought causes my lips to tremble, but I push it away and focus again on the surrounding forest.

Instead of embarrassing myself by breaking down, I turn the conversation into something more solid.

"Why did they decide to build the houses into the trees?" I ask, gazing out over the expanse.

"Some think these trees are sacred. The legend is that the Green Man once lived here and granted the trees protection and immortality. It is said that these trees have been here for one thousand years and will remain for another thousand."

They are five times larger than any other tree I have seen, and it is easy to believe they are invincible.

"Who is the Green Man?"

My curiosity about this mysterious, mythical man is piqued. I always loved hearing fairy tales from my nanny growing up, and I would often beg her for story after story before she put me to bed.

"He is the man of the forest. Responsible for rebirth and seasonal renewal. See," he says, pointing to a totem pole a few yards from where we stand.

The base of the pole has vines and leaves carved into it. At the top is the image of a man's head with vines pouring out his mouth and nostrils. It is a beautiful depiction, and my fingers itched to run them over the intricate details.

"That is the mayday pole." Rowan continues. "We gather there to celebrate the beginning of summer and give thanks to the Green Man for the bountiful season."

In my mind, I can picture the celebration happening in the square below. Ribbons tied around the Maypole and children winding them around as their laughter floats through the air. We never celebrated May Day, but I have heard about it, and look forward to seeing the festivities.

That is if I am here that long.

A few stray birds dart through the trees, chasing each other as they weave through the branches and soar above the treetops.

I can see the appeal of living up high like this and wish we could stay up here forever and gaze out over the forest. I feel like a bird, perched up high in its nest and gazing out across the forest floor, happy in its knowledge that it is out of reach of most predators.

"Why don't you live up here in one of the trees?"

His sheepish expression piques my curiosity.

"Tell me," I say, pulling on his hand with a grin.

“It’s the swaying of the trees. It makes me feel ill.”

I can’t help the burst of laughter that escapes me.

“I would think the motion of the trees is relaxing, not sickening.”

“Go ahead and laugh. Everyone else thinks me silly as well.”

I like that about him. It makes it easier thinking of him with a flaw. Even a minor one.

I move closer to him and lean an arm against him, enjoying the warmth of him for one precious moment.

A boy walks below the platform with a basket of mushrooms and I shudder as I recall the hallucinations they invoked. It makes me sad and a little ashamed that this entire community can thrive off self-sustainability and I couldn’t even make it half a day without nearly killing myself.

Rowan notices me eyeing the mushrooms and touches my arm gently. “I could teach you, you know. How to gather. How to survive. Here. With us.”

When I look at him, his eyes are gentle. It seems he is imploring me to say yes.

My eyebrows knit together in confusion. Time and time again this man has gone out of his way to help me. What could he possibly have to gain by these acts of kindness?

"Why are you helping me?"

"I have my reasons," he says with that damn lopsided grin that makes my legs weak.

Indecision weighs heavily on me, and I swallow a lump in my throat as I attempt to sort out my thoughts. Am I ready to trust this man so easily? Perhaps I should keep traveling until I have put more distance between my mother and myself. Would I even survive if I attempted to leave again? The thoughts swirl round and round. One question morphing into two and then ten and then one hundred.

I try to stay neutral and weigh the benefits of staying versus leaving but this place is already burrowing itself inside my heart. This place and this man.

"All right, Little Bird, come along then. We have people to meet."

He grabs my hand and begins tugging me along. His hand is warm around mine and every so often he squeezes it gently. I don't know if he is trying to reassure himself that I am still here or the other way around, but I smile every time I feel that tightening of his fingers around mine.

He leads me across several more bridges, weaving in and out of trees and over branches. At last, we come to a house set high up in the embrace of a massive oak tree. He knocks on the arched doorframe but enters before the person inside has a chance to respond.

"Oh, Rowan," a woman says. "Come take the babe while I finish up this pudding."

When she turns, I notice she bears a striking resemblance to Rowan with her chestnut hair and large amber eyes. She carries a baby on her hip and bounces him while trying to stir a pot one-handed. Rowan walks forward to pick up the baby and cradles him in his arms. He blows raspberries on the boy's chubby cheeks, causing the baby to giggle.

"Anastasia, is it?" The woman asks as she moves towards me and wipes her hands on her apron. She extends her hand to me and when I shake it, she clasps her other hand over mine. She gives me such a genuine smile, that I can't help but smile back.

"No, Mom," Ewin says from beside her. "Remember what I told you earlier. Her name is Anya now."

He rolls his eyes as if exasperated at having to tell her a second time.

"Well, it is wonderful to meet you, Anya. I'm Lynet," she says with a wink. "I'm glad to see the dress fits."

"Yes. And I hear you are also to thank for the wonderful meal I indulged in earlier. That was by far the most delicious thing I have ever eaten."

She blushes at my praise and takes her hand back.

"It was nothing but I'm glad you enjoyed it. Perhaps if you stay a bit longer, I can interest you in some pudding?"

Another little boy pulls on my arm, demanding my attention.

"Mommy makes it with apples and cinnamon, and it is my favorite thing in the whole world," he insists.

"Well, it certainly smells wonderful. And who might you be?" I ask, kneeling so I am at eye level with the child.

"I am Jacob. I was the youngest until mom had another baby. Now I am a big brother and get to boss him around, like my brothers do to me."

He has the same blonde curls as his siblings, but his eyes are blue whereas the other children's eyes are amber, like their mothers.

"It is a pleasure to meet you, Jacob. I am Anya. A friend of your uncle Rowan."

"Are you his girlfriend?" He giggles into his hand.

"No, we are just friends. Your uncle saved my life when I ate something I shouldn't have."

"What did you eat?" Ewin asks.

"A mushroom."

Jacob rolls his eyes and throws his hands up in the air in exasperation.

"Everyone knows you don't eat mushrooms without asking your mom first."

"Well, now I know," I reply. "I haven't had anyone teach me about such things, but your uncle Rowan promises to teach me all about plants if I decide to stay."

"I hope you stay," Ewin says, suddenly turning shy and hiding behind his mom's dress.

"I hope she stays too," Rowan says with a grin. "Now how about that pudding? I haven't eaten in over two hours. I am likely to starve if I don't eat something soon."

"Oh, you," Lynet says, swatting Rowan with a dishtowel. "Go sit at the table and I'll bring it over shortly."

"Where is your other son?" I ask, noticing one of the three I saw earlier is missing.

"I sent him hunting with his father. I needed a bit of quiet in the house and he needs to practice his archery skills."

The two remaining boys begin to wrestle, toppling each other to the ground and knocking over a small table. Luckily, the table didn't sustain much damage, and the boys are led outside by their ears.

"A lot of good that did me," she huffs. "Three boys can make just as much noise as four."

Realizing she has her hands full, I ask, "Can I help with anything?"

“If you don’t mind stirring this pudding for a few moments, I need to lay the baby down for his nap.”

As if on cue, the baby lets out a wail that no amount of leg bouncing or hushing will quiet.

I walk to the stove and pick up the spoon, suddenly nervous. I have never cooked anything and this task suddenly seems daunting.

I pick up the spoon and glance over my shoulder to ensure she isn't watching before beginning. Staring down at the bubbling mixture in the pot, I shrug. How hard can it be?

Grabbing the handle of the pot, I immediately realize it is a mistake. The handle is scalding hot, and I nearly topple the entire kettle off the stove before snatching my hand back.

“Bloody hell,” I yell out. Luckily, I removed it fast enough that it won't blister, but it hurts like hell, and I blow on it to keep the pain down.

“Here,” Rowan says.

He reaches his arms around me, caging me in between his body and the stove. Grasping my hand, he brings it to his mouth and blows softly on it before placing a kiss on my palm. The feeling of his lips on my skin is enough to distract me from the pain, and my eyes linger on his lips when he pulls back. His touch is intoxicating.

It's like he has some hold over me, and no matter how hard I try, every thought morphs into thoughts of him touching me, kissing me, deep inside me. Okay, stop. Control your wayward thoughts for five minutes. Geesh.

I shake my head and breathe deeply as he turns me back to the stove and stands directly behind me. Focus on the pudding.

He holds a dish rag in his hand and grabs the handle while handing me the spoon.

"Try again, Little Bird."

His breath tickles the hair on my neck, and a shiver runs down the length of my body as he leans in closer.

"Like this," he says, taking my hand in his.

With our hands combined, he stirs the pudding with slow, languid movements. It takes everything in me not to back up the few inches that separate us, molding my body to his. Even with the space between us, I can feel the heat of his body through my clothes. So close.

"Uh hum," Lynet says, clearing her voice behind us.

I turn so quickly that I accidentally knock the spoon out of the pot, and it clatters to the floor with a mess of pudding.

"I'm so sorry," I say quickly, kneeling to clean up the mess. "I didn't mean... I burned my... He was just..." I let the words trail off, not bothering to finish the sentence. I am beyond mortified. After all she has done to extend kindness to me, I am in her kitchen with her brother, having impure thoughts of him throwing me down on her table and having his way with me.

Dear lord. Please help me.

Lynet kneels and helps me wipe up the mess before addressing me. “Anastasia. Please look at me.”

With my cheeks still blazing with heat, I look up and see only kindness reflected in her gaze.

“It's okay. I'm glad Rowan has a friend he can finally be comfortable with. You will find no judgment from me or anyone else in this town. We only want the people here to be happy.” She looks over at her brother with a sly smile. “And it appears you make my brother happy.”

“Lynet,” Rowan says with exasperation.

“Well, she does. A sister can tell. It's about time you found happiness after all this time.”

It's on the tip of my tongue to ask what she means by that, but I bite back the words. How is it possible he hasn’t already settled down with a wife? I am curious but don’t want to appear rude for asking.

“Thank you, Lynet. For everything. You have been so kind.”

“Think nothing of it,” she says, taking the soiled rags from me. “Now, let's have some of this pudding.”

We sit at the table to enjoy the dessert, and I realize Jacob is right. The combination of apples and cinnamon makes this one of the most delicious things I have ever tasted.

As the minutes of easy conversation tick by, I forget my embarrassment and sink into the happy comradery. For the first time in years, I feel something other than loneliness.

Chapter 8.

That night, I wake up in a cold sweat, clawing at my blankets to escape the nightmare that followed me into reality. Even as I tell myself repeatedly that it was all a dream, I can picture every detail with terrifying clarity.

That horrible, maniacal laugh. The dungeon. Reginald's hands. It is too much, and I can't catch my breath as the images play over again. The terror claws at my chest, and my body shakes uncontrollably with unspent adrenaline.

Before I know what is happening, Rowan is pulling me into his arms while I sob against his chest. His warm body wraps around me, and he strokes my damp hair away from my face in slow, rhythmic movements.

"Shhh, it was only a dream, Anya. You are safe now."

His voice soothes my frantic mind, and I am desperate to hear him say my name again. Even though Ewin designated my new nickname with childish innocence, the sound of it brings me back to the present. I am no longer Anastasia. That girl has been left behind in the castle. I have changed these last few days. The spark inside me has begun to burn hot in my chest, and I am desperate to keep that flame alive.

"Say it again," I beg.

"Which part?" he asks, soothing my damp hair away from my forehead.

"All of it. Any of it. I need to hear your voice."

"Anya, my sweet Little Bird."

My muscles begin to relax, and I lay my head on his lap as he strokes my hair. He continues, talking in soothing whispers that feel like a balm against my racing heart. He says something in Latin that sounds like a poem, and even though I can't understand the words, it sounds peaceful. He repeats it before switching to English so I can understand.

"A bird with broken wings can only go so far.

Most nights, her only comfort is to wish upon a star.

At times, she feels the weakest and anything but strong,

She remembers that the darkest days can only last so long.

The weeks and months float away,

And finally comes the day,

She spreads her mended wings out wide,

And lets the wind carry her away."

His words calm me, and soon, the crushing terror of my dreams sinks into the back of my mind. I reach up and lay a hand on his arm, relishing the feel of his skin beneath my fingers.

"That is beautiful. Where did you hear it?" I ask.

"My mother used to sing it to me when I was young. It made me think of you the first time I saw you."

"And that's why you call me Little Bird?"

"Yes. You may be Anya to Ewin but will always be Little Bird to me."

The moonlight coming in through the window casts his face in profile, and I marvel at the sharp lines of his face, itching to run my fingers across that stubbled jaw.

The darkness provides a cloak of anonymity, which makes me feel brave. The mixture of that and the burning low in my stomach are a lethal combination.

I want him.

This man is turning me into someone else. Someone who feels brave and strong. Someone who is not afraid to take what they want and hell with the consequences. I want him. And if the glimmer in his eye is an indication, he wants me to.

The temptation to press my lips to his is irresistible, and before I can think better of it, I do it.

I pull his head down and claim his mouth.

Every muscle in his body goes taught when our lips meet, but I can feel the second he relaxes and slants his mouth over mine to deepen our kiss. His tongue slides inside my mouth, and I bite back a moan at the delicious taste of him. He breaks away, and I note with some satisfaction that his eyes are burning with desire, and his breathing is ragged.

His hands dig into my hair, and he angles my head again to trail kisses down my neck.

He hovers over my bodice momentarily, nipping at the fabric with his teeth before returning to my mouth. Heat pools between my thighs as he continues his assault on my lips, and a moan escapes my throat. This moment seems like the most exquisite torture while I wait for his body to claim mine.

I need it. Now. I need him.

I become impatient and push at the hem of his shirt, wanting to feel more of him. He grabs my hands and, with a deep sigh, pulls away. I can feel his heartbeat beneath my hands, and it beats at the same frantic pace as my own.

"It is selfish of me to want you to stay. But I do. I love having you here, in my house. In my bed. In my life. But I want you to decide whether you will stay before this goes any further. Your touch will break me, Anya, and I don't know if I can handle you leaving me after I have had you."

I want to scream out. Yes! I want to stay, but something holds me back, even now. The life we could have flashes before my eyes, intermingled with the life I left behind. How can such happiness be possible when I have felt such sorrow?

In what world can two such opposite emotions ever live in the same life? The truth is, I am scared. I'm afraid to allow myself to be happy and scared to have that much hope for my future.

"Take your time deciding, Little Bird. Just know that you will be mine if you decide to stay."

I feel as if my heart is breaking as he places the lightest of kisses on my lips before moving away. Everything inside of me is screaming to say yes. I will stay. But that niggling fear works itself inside my brain like a worm. Planting doubt and fear as it passes. I wish my brain would turn off for one moment. Put an end to this constant worrying and let myself sink into the freedom I have dreamt of for so long. Blowing out a deep breath, I mentally kick my overactive brain for foiling what could have been an unforgettable night.

Rowan lays back down on the floor, and I try to fall asleep but lie awake with my eyes wide open, replaying the last few minutes in my mind. I touch my lips, wishing his lips were still there.

I whisper, "That was a hell of a first kiss, Rowan."

He chuckles from his makeshift bed. I didn't think he would hear me, but I'm not sorry he heard. It's true. My lips still tingle from the memory of his lips on mine, and it takes every ounce of restraint not to leap off the bed and throw myself at him.

I toss and turn, unable to find sleep again after my adrenaline has been activated. First, the nightmare, and then that kiss.

Pushing the blankets back, I give up on any attempts to sleep. Snow is beginning to fall outside, and I stand up to get a better view through the pane of glass. Lights burn in the distance, moving through the trees at a steady pace. Condensation has developed on the glass from the cold, and I wipe it away, trying to make out where the lights are coming from.

"They are celebrating." The noise comes from behind my right ear, and I practically jump out of my skin at the nearness. I place a hand over my heart and swat at Rowan's chest.

"You scared me to death. I didn't hear you get up."

He lets out a deep chuckle, which immediately sends heat straight between my thighs.

Dear lord. Even his laugh can arouse me. This man is dangerous.

"They are holding a ceremony for the winter solstice. They get together to celebrate the rising of the new sun."

"The new sun?"

"Yes. The new sun brings warmth and life, leaving the shortest days behind and moving towards a time of life."

"Why aren't you celebrating with them?"

"I didn't want to leave you," he replies sheepishly.

Instead of telling him that is nonsense, that I will be fine by myself I ask, "Can I come with you?"

"Are you sure? You may not understand much of what is said or happens."

"Do they sacrifice people?" I ask, grimacing.

He lets out a bark of laughter. "They do not sacrifice people or even animals, for that matter."

"Then let's go. Please." I let the last word drag out for several seconds and pull on his hand, leading him to the door. I probably sound like a begging child, but I don't care. The prospect of a celebration excites me, and I hold my breath while I wait for his response.

"Oh, all right. Let's put on cloaks and hats, though. We will be out there until dawn."

"Yes!" I exclaim, quickly pulling on my cloak.

When we step outside, the cold air nearly steals my breath. The temperature has plummeted since the sun set, and I bury my hands deep inside my pockets to keep them warm.

The snow crunches beneath our feet, and I exhale puffs of white. Even with the colder temperatures, my excitement grows the closer we get to the lights. The forest opens to a large clearing where dozens of people stand in a circle, holding hands and chanting. The voices are perfectly synchronized as they speak in a language I cannot understand. It sends a chill up my spine to hear the foreign tongue, and I can only guess what they are saying.

Another circle of villagers is on the outskirts of the clearing, holding up the torches I saw from the window. They stay silent and hold their lights up high.

There must be close to one hundred people in attendance, and I marvel at the serenity exuded by this large group of onlookers. The children, bundled up beneath thick wool blankets, are also quiet during the ceremony.

Rosy cheeks and noses peek out from the layers of clothing while they wait patiently for the ceremony to end.

The chant is beautiful, and they repeat it several times before breaking apart. Now that the inner circle has dispersed, the ceremony is complete, and the celebration can begin.

A few women walk forward to light a large bonfire in the middle of the clearing. It only takes moments before the huge pyre is engulfed in flames, and the air around us immediately becomes warmer.

The fire spits and crackles as it consumes the wood, and before long, the fire is so tall it nearly touches the overhanging branches. Fiery embers float up into the sky, and the sky now resembles a mass of fireflies shooting off into the night.

Heat spreads through my body, and I hold my hands out to the flames, relishing how it warms my skin.

I never had enough wood in the dungeon, and this excess of heat seems like an impossibly delicious luxury.

Rowan grabs my hand and leads me to a bench where we can sit and enjoy the festive atmosphere while staying close to the heat.

Groups of people walk about, laughing and contributing to the joyous mood. I want to get up and join in their banter but suddenly feel shy in my new surroundings. What could I possibly say to them? Hello. My name is Anastasia, and I have been locked up in a dungeon for the last ten years by my mother. I think not. The only person I have conversed with for all those solitary years was a wolf whose uncommunicative side of the conversation was less than engaging.

Rowan wraps an arm around my waist and leans into me. I give him a watery smile as I try to bolster my spirits and gather the courage to introduce myself to the people here.

When he turns to face me, the firelight is flickering in the reflection of his eyes.

At least, I think the fire is causing that heat in his gaze. His eyes fall to my mouth, and he traces a finger over my bottom lip.

"I can't forget the taste of you," he whispers.

My mouth goes dry, and the ever-present burning between my thighs intensifies. The memory of his tongue sweeping over mine invades my memory. I'm tempted to reach up and kiss him again, but a loud bark of laughter interrupts the moment.

The laughter came from a large, burly man, passing a jug from one person to the next.

He makes his way to us and holds up the jug.

"Would you care for something to warm you up, lass?" the man says in a thick Scottish brogue. His thick red beard can't mask his rosy cheeks and the smile that goes from ear to ear.

"I would love that," I reply.

I'm not even remotely sure of what I am agreeing to, but decide to be brave and try something new.

"Are you sure?" Rowan asks with raised eyebrows. "Old man Duncan's whiskey can pack quite a punch."

"I'm sure," I respond confidently. How bad can it be?

As soon as the liquid fire enters my mouth, I realize my mistake.

I swallow despite the burning and realize that swallowing makes it worse. Much worse. I begin coughing despite my best efforts to appear unaffected, and Duncan pats me on the back with a hearty laugh.

"Oh, she's a keeper, Rowan." He winks. "Would you care for another swig, my lady?"

"Maybe later," I croak, still trying to control my coughing.

"How about you, Rowan?"

"Aye, I'll have a wee nip," Rowan replies, mimicking the old man's Scottish brogue. Duncan laughs and slaps him on the back as Rowan takes a deep drink.

His eyes water a bit, but he doesn't have nearly the visceral reaction that I had.

"Best yet, Duncan. We will come find you when the lass is ready for another go." Rowan says, handing him back the jug.

I elbow him in the ribs but can't help the laughter from bubbling up. The whiskey did warm my insides quite nicely.

"Now what?" I ask, unsure of what usually happens during a winter solstice celebration.

"Now," he whispers in my ear, "we sit and wait for the sun to come up over the horizon."

"That's it?"

"That's it," he confirms.

"What makes this night so special?"

"It is the longest night of the year. These people value life above all else. The new sun brings life, and we must pay our due respect."

"To a god?" I ask, confused.

"Not a God necessarily. For years, we have lived in the trees and kept to ourselves. Some call us Druids. Others say we worship any number of Gods or Goddesses, but the truth is that we simply worship nature. The waxing and waning of the moon. The stars above our heads. The food which we consume. We respect and are thankful for all of it. Most think it is a religion, but it is just a way of life."

His words resonate deep inside my soul, and I am at a loss for words. Every religion I have heard of has fought for what they believe in. Murder and rules, Purging and brimstone. But a way of life that simply existed to give thanks? I don't know what to say to that.

We stand there, watching for the first tinge of daylight to peak over the horizon. The crowd has quieted, and everyone has their faces pointed towards the sky, just waiting.

It is a peaceful pause. The forest seems to be holding its breath as it waits with the rest of us.

Rowan grasps my hand in his and tucks it inside his pocket. His thumb strokes lazy circles over the back of my hand as we wait. The first rays of sun over the hill are met with a collective sigh, followed by a murmur. It begins as a faint orange glow that slowly emerges above the horizon. Hues of purple and pink transform to a brilliant yellow as they crest the final few inches to shine down richly on our faces. The moment it breaks free from the horizon, the entire crowd bows their head and steeples their hands.

"Awen," they say in unison.

"Awen?" I ask, looking at Rowan, who is participating in the procession. "Is that like Amen?"

"It means, thank you."

"Thank you to the earth?"

"Yes, in a sense."

From my limited experience, it always seemed like people were cold and calculating, only doing something they could benefit from. But here, everyone is so warm and open.

The thought of staying here permanently enters my mind, but I brush it away quickly. Several times, I have avoided entertaining the notion to save my heart from breaking wide open.

To admit that I want to stay here would admit to myself that this could be my future. Could I dare to dream about what my future could hold? I have never allowed myself to think about more than the next day for fear that my hopes would be dashed. But here, perhaps I can hope. Hope that my future will be as bright and happy as the faces that surround me. Hope that I can learn to gather knowledge about the forest and how to prepare my own meals. Hope that this man looking at me with such tenderness, even now, might care for me. Perhaps one day, even love me.

At that moment, Duncan returns through the crowd and holds up his nearly empty jug. "How about another splash of the old fire liquid?" he asks in a slightly slurred voice.

I laugh at him as he uncorks it and takes a healthy swig for himself.

"Oh, why not? You only live once." This earns me a slap on the back and an approving smile.

Chapter 9.

The next few days fly by in a flurry of new faces and experiences I have only ever dreamed of.

All of Rowan's sisters stop in to meet me and while their company is wonderful, I struggle to keep all the names and faces straight. There are just so many of them.

Lynet, whom I have already met, stops by several times with fresh bread and a few other staples to tide us over. She is the oldest and secretly my favorite. Although they are all warm and caring, something about Lynet pulls at my heart.

Then, there is Celeste, the youngest sister, and her husband, Bruce. They don't have any children yet, but Celeste has a bump protruding from under her dress that suggests she will be a mother in the next few months.

Next is Ella, who is only a year older than Celeste. Ella has five-year-old twins. A boy, named Dax, and a girl, named Amara. Her husband, William, is a hunter and is often away for several days at a time. He and a handful of others supply the town with most of the meat.

Last is Joy, the second eldest sister, and her two children, Emma and Freya. She has a hand held to a small bump on her stomach that shows a third child is on its way. Her husband, Simon, is on a week-long hunting trip but should be returning any day.

Both her daughters are adorable with long brown hair and big doe eyes. They are weary of me at first but soon warm up to my presence and sit on my lap while Rowan and his sister talk.

At one point Emma grabs a book and holds it up to me, asking if I can read them a story. Unsure of what to say, I open the book and my face flushes hot with embarrassment when only a few words on the page look familiar to me

Although it is not uncommon for people to not know how to read, when you are surrounded by others who can, it makes you feel like you are somehow lacking.

Only moments ago, I had felt so at home here and growing comfortable with the idea of staying. Now, self-consciousness creeps back in and makes me feel like an imposter trying to force something that isn't meant to be. Rowan laughs heartily at something Joy says, and the pure joy on his face makes me feel that much worse for trying to insert myself into his life. Everything he has here is so perfect and unencumbered. Then I come along with my nightmares and lack of knowledge. What can I possibly offer this man that another woman couldn't tenfold? Surely, there is a better fit for him somewhere. He is too perfect for the likes of me, and I should just sulk off in the night while he is not looking. He would be better off without me. I'm sure of it.

Joy notices my sudden discomfort and scoops one of the little girls in her arms.

"We must be on our way now, but it was lovely meeting you, Anya," Joy says, ushering the two girls to the door.

"It was wonderful to meet you also. And thank you again for the wonderful cloak. I'm sorry I have nothing to give you in return."

"You are most welcome. We take care of our own here," she says with a wink before exiting the house.

Our own... Does that mean they have accepted me into their town so readily? A lump forms in my throat, and I swallow it down as tears prick the corners of my eyes.

Rowan seems to pick up on the fact that my heart is heavy.

"Would you like to spend the day in the forest? We won't be able to gather as much as we would in the spring and summer, but a few perennials still grow in winter."

"I would love that," I say, inconspicuously wiping the unshed tears from my eyes.

"Here, let me help you with that," he says, wrapping my new cloak around my shoulders and tying it with skilled fingers. His fingers linger on the skin at the base of my throat, and my heartbeat grows erratic at his touch. He is close. Too close. His lips would be on mine if I stand on tiptoes and lean in a few inches. The thought suddenly consumes me, and he licks his lips as if anticipating the kiss as much as me. But instead of kissing me, he brushes his thumb over my lips and leans in to whisper in my ear.

"I'm happy you came." His breath tickles my ear, and a shiver of pleasure cascades down my spine.

"I'm glad you found me," I reply, grasping onto his arms as he leans back.

"Are you ready?"

I nod, unable to gather my breath to respond when he looks at me like this. It seems like he wants to devour me, and he licks his lips again before sighing and turning away.

Grabbing his cloak, we leave the house and venture into the forest.

The scent of pine trees surrounds us as we move farther into the trees. Only a few plants grow at this time of the year, and we have to search to find anything we can harvest. We gather pine needles for tea and willow bark, which he tells me is a potent pain killer. He crests a small hill and lets out a cry of astonishment when he sees what is on the other side. I stand beside him but see nothing that would be cause for excitement.

"What is it?" I whisper.

"Ginseng. See the small red berries surrounded by the five green leaves?"

"What does it do?" I ask, screwing up my eyebrows in confusion.

"It is rare in these parts. The roots are used for many different remedies. Lugh will certainly be happy if we bring back a basket of these for him."

"Who is Lugh?"

"He is the town wise man and healer. He specializes in the more difficult remedies and uses Ginseng in many of them whenever it can be found.

Rowan pulls a tool out of his bag with a flat stone head on one end and a long wooden handle.

"It's a spade," he says when he notices me eyeing the tool warily. "We would normally dig the roots by hand, but the ground is a bit stiff with cold, and we will need this to dig them up."

And that's just what we do. We spend the next few hours harvesting Ginseng roots and saving the berries for replanting. Rowan does the digging and hands me the roots, which I clean off before storing them inside a sack.

When we finish, we have a bag stuffed full of the precious roots. We both smell of moss and earth from digging. Rowan has dirt covering his hands and forehead. I laugh at his dirty appearance.

"What is so funny?" he asks.

"You have dirt everywhere. Even on your face."

"Oh, and you think you are without your filthy face?"

He reaches up and smears a dirty thumb across my cheek, leaving a trail of mud behind.

"Hey!" I yell at him and reach out to leave my own mark on his face.

I squeal in shock as he picks up a handful of dirt from the ground and looks at me with a devilish glint in his eye.

"Don't you dare," I warn.

"I'll give you a three-second head start."

With a squeal of fright, I take off towards town, jumping over fallen logs and laughing as I run. Rowan is only a few steps behind me, and he collides with my back when I stop suddenly, nearly sending us both to the ground.

"What did you stop for?" he asks curiously.

I can't speak. My words are frozen in my throat. All I can do is point.

On the trail ahead of us is a wolf. But this is not the wolf I previously encountered. This one is so skinny I can see his ribs poking out through his fur, and a row of savage teeth are staring back at us as he snarls and snaps. Drool is dripping from his quivering lips as he advances towards us.

Terror threatens to consume me, and I search the area for a weapon. A sharp branch or large stone which I might use to protect myself. I find nothing. My heart sinks even farther when three more wolves slink out from the trees, flanking the leader on each side.

"Back up slowly," Rowan instructs, keeping his voice low.

I do as he says, and he moves in front of me to block me from the advancing threat. I peek around his body to see what is happening but immediately wish I hadn't. My body shakes so hard I can almost hear my bones rattling, but Rowan is eerily calm. How in the world is he not panicking right now? Those wolves will tear us to shreds.

"Should we run?" I whisper, trying unsuccessfully to keep my voice from shaking.

"No. Hold perfectly still."

It takes every ounce of energy to do as he asks, but I close my eyes and prepare myself for the death that is undoubtedly coming. Those hungry beasts won't let an easy meal out of their grasp, that much is for sure. We are going to die here. Just when I finally found an ounce of freedom, it will be ripped away in an instant.

I scream in terror when a wolf lunges for us, and I fall backward, holding my arms over my face in a pathetic attempt to defend myself.

But the blow never comes.

Instead, a clash of teeth meets my ears instead of the screams of pain I had anticipated. When my hands finally unclench from in front of my face, I peek through my fingers and survey the destruction around me.

A pile of fur and clashing teeth command my attention but I can't determine one wolf from the next. Through all the savagery, a black wolf emerges from the thick of the snarling pile.

My wolf.

How did he find us? It is then that I realize I am alone, other than the fighting wolves.

Rowan is gone.

Where in the world did he go? I search left and right, trying to find his broken body on the ground or amid the fight, but he is nowhere to be found.

"Rowan," I yell.

When I call Rowan's name, the black wolf looks at me briefly, but it is enough for the pack's leader to lunge and sink his teeth into his shoulder.

A howl of pain pierces the night air as blood sprays out from the wound. Another wolf pounces, grabs ahold of his leg, and pulls at it savagely, leaving behind long gouges where his teeth sunk in.

The black wolf is outnumbered and injured, but he isn't giving up on the fight just yet. His teeth wrap around the leader's throat and rips open the tender flesh, causing a fatal blow if ever there was one. The leader slumps onto the ground, pouring his remaining lifeblood onto the leaves and soaking the ground with his blood. He whimpers once before his head falls to the ground, and his sightless eyes stare straight at me.

The three other wolves soon meet a similar fate without the strength of their alpha and are soon strewn about the ground, lifeless and destroyed.

A whimper leaves my lips, and I attempt to stand but crumple back into a heap on the ground. Silent tears are streaking down my cheeks, and I cry out again.

"Rowan, where are you? Please answer me." I search the surrounding area frantically but come up empty.

The black wolf walks to me, panting and bloody from the fight. He lays down in front of me and places his head on the earth near my feet. A whimper escapes him as I take in the destruction of his body. I reach for the raw flesh on his shoulder but think better of touching a wounded animal and pull my fingers back before they make contact.

Blood oozes from the jagged cuts, and I hesitate for only a brief moment longer before ripping the hem off my dress and attempting to staunch the flow of blood. When I push down, a snarl escapes his throat before he mercifully slumps down into unconsciousness. With my hand pressed against the wound, I survey the area again, desperate to find Rowan. Where could he have gone? I don't understand. He couldn't have just vanished into thin air.

A twig snaps behind me, and I turn my head to look, but nothing is there. The trees are the only observers of my desperate pleas. The forest suddenly seems too large and I whimper as my mind goes blank. *Think Anya, Think.* He couldn't have just vanished.

And then the strangest thing happens. The wolf begins to change. At first, it is only small things. His fur seems too smooth, and his ears look slightly smaller. Then, the changes begin to become more apparent. Flesh begins to emerge from the thick black coat of fur, and his canine face morphs into something different. Something like Rowan. I stare in disbelief at the sight before me, even as the transformation twists and changes all the pieces until they fit together perfectly. Then, all that remains is Rowan. He lies before me, bleeding and unconscious. Shallow breaths leave his body, and he twitches like he is in the middle of a nightmare.

Only then do I let out a scream. The scream is so loud it sends a flock of birds shooting off the trees above us. I scream again, letting the loud visceral noise ground me. This can't be real. The only other inkling of magic I had was that swirling blue orb in my mother's bedroom, but even that had begun to fade from my memory.

But this?

This is beyond anything I ever imagined might exist. How can this possibly be? And why did he not tell me? I have spent time with him. Lived with him even, but no hint of him being something other than human ever occurred to me.

I stand up and begin to back away from him. This can't be Rowan. Not the Rowan I know.

I turn and run into the forest, wanting to leave this nightmare behind me. Why? Why is this happening? I finally found a sliver of happiness, and now everything has been turned on its head once again.

A noise stops me in my tracks. A cry of pain. Fuck. The memory of those amber eyes, imploring me to stay, returns to me. I brace my hands on my knees and take several deep breaths. Squeezing my eyes shut, I grit my teeth and turn back around.

This is a bad idea. I should just keep running until I find somewhere safe. Somewhere where I can just be an ordinary woman, falling for a normal man. But no. I had to go and fall for a man who is a fricken wolf shifter. Another cry of pain spurs me into action, and I straighten my back and raise my head. I can see him in the clearing, writhing in agony on the ground. And the sight strengthens my resolve. I know that I can't leave him.

Walking tentatively back to where he is, I crouch beside him and lay a hand on his back.

Breathing in through my nose, I take in his broken body again and push all other thoughts away. Okay, so he is a wolf. A wolf, man. A shapeshifter. Werewolf? What the hell he happens to be, he is also hurt. Badly. And I need to find a way to help.

"Rowan," I say, slapping his cheek to get his attention. "Rowan," I say louder when that fails to generate a response. His eyes are squeezed shut, and his teeth are clenched so tightly that spittle has formed at the corners of his mouth.

Finally, as a last-ditch effort to rouse him, I squeeze the fabric around his shoulder. This causes him to moan before he turns over and vomits in the dirt.

"Fuck, that hurts," he says through half-closed lids.

"I am not going to dwell on the fact that you lied to me, but we need to have a serious discussion about what just happened," I say.

I attempt to lift him up. This proves harder than I thought since he weighs considerably more than me, and my muscles protest as I lift and heave with all my strength. I manage to prop him up into a very undignified slump, and my heart beats wildly in my chest from the exertion.

Maybe I should just fetch help and return with a few strong men. But the blood seeping out of his wounds tells me I need to act now, and the trek to town and back will take too long. He might not last that long.

Grunting, I place my hands under his armpits and pull. He grunts but finally gets his uninjured leg under him and pushes himself into a standing position with a string of expletives. His hair is damp with sweat, and he leans heavily against me as he catches his breath. The scent of blood and sweat swirls around me, but I don't have time to dwell on that now. I need to get him moving.

"For the record, I didn't lie," he says through gritted teeth as he takes his first few steps. Sweat trails down his temple as he tries walking through the pain.

Along with the gash on his shoulder, blood is soaking through his pant leg, and a piece of his earlobe is torn in half and will require stitches. The blood from his ear slides down his shoulder and onto my arm, but I don't let myself focus on the crimson liquid. If I am to get him back home, I can't allow myself to dwell on the sight of that blood.

"As a matter of fact, you did lie to me," I say, trying to keep him talking.

“When?" he asks, taking a few more pained steps. If we progress at this pace, it will take us an eternity to return.

"When I asked you about the wolf that first day we met. You said he comes and goes as he pleases but omitted the fact that the wolf is you."

"Still not a lie, Little Bird," his cocky grin momentarily eases my fear, and I almost laugh. That is before he trips over a covered root, sending us both staggering forward. Luckily, I catch him before he falls, but the pained look on his face and the blood soaking through his clothing urges me into action.

I kneel down and rip another two strips from my dress. Taking a deep breath, I look up at him. "I'm sorry," I tell him before pulling the strips tight around his leg. He lets out an agonized cry and nearly collapses on top of me, but I grab him just in time and hug him to my body to keep him upright. His muscles are quivering and he buries his face in my neck as his tremors subside.

Finally, he takes a deep breath and leans his forehead against mine. I kiss him. Not a passionate kiss. Just a brush of my lips against his for support. His lips are still quivering slightly, but he drags in a deep breath, and we turn to continue our way back to the village.

"Lean against me more," I tell him.

"I'll crush you," he insists, trying and failing to make it another two steps.

"I said, lean on me. Now," I say, demanding as much conviction into my voice as I can muster.

He complies, mostly out of fatigue, but I use it to my advantage. My knees threaten to buckle under his weight as he leans heavily on me and drapes an arm around me. I begin walking, and every muscle protests against the extra weight. In a few hundred feet, I realize we are in trouble.

Perspiration breaks out along my body as my muscles are forced to endure much more than they are capable of.

But I refuse to fall.

I count my steps and fixate on a new milestone with each new patch of forest that comes into view. *Just make it to that large rock. Now, the gnarled oak tree. You only must make it to the patch of grass over there. And finally, that ladder affixed to the tree. A ladder! Finally. We made it back to the clearing.* It feels like an eternity has passed, and Rowan is now more unconscious than conscious. I drag him the last few yards into the village. My legs burn, and as soon as we pass into the clearing of the Dark Forest, I begin to yell.

"Lynet," I scream, hoping she is home. "Please, Lynet. Rowan needs help."

I see one small face poke through the doorway, followed by another and another. The children's shocked faces soon turn into tears, and they begin to cry as they clamber down the ladder.

"Mommy, Mommy. Rowan is hurt."

Next comes Lynet, walking through the door and wiping her hands on her apron. "What in the..." But her words are cut off when she sees her brother's broken body on the path below. Every ounce of color drains from her face at that moment.

She runs back into the house and merges seconds later with a basket slung over her arm.

She descends the ladder at an unnatural speed and races towards us. The children surround her, grasping at her dress with tears streaming down their faces. A lady from a nearby house comes to usher the children away, whispering reassurances into their ears.

However, the glance she throws over her shoulder betrays her words. Her eyes contact mine briefly, and it seems she is telling me to prepare for the worst.

"Anya," Lynet urges. "We need to get him home. He can't climb the ladder like this and is too large for us to carry up. Help me get him on his feet."

Her words shake me out of my fear-driven stupor, and I crouch preparing to lift him. My muscles scream at me and threaten to give out, but we finally manage to get him standing. His head lolls to the side, and his lids remain closed as we half carry him to his house. Sweat is beading on my forehead by the time we finally manage to cross the threshold, and I grit my teeth to keep back the tears of pain and fear.

We ungracefully drop him onto the bed and take a second to gather our breath. Our chests are heaving, and Lynet's hair has come undone from her bun. She pushes a few strands back from her face and closes her eyes for only a moment. Taking one steadying breath, she says." Okay. I need to cut off his clothes to bandage the injuries. We will need hot water and cloth for binding. Can you help with that, Anya?"

"Yes," I answer quickly.

I have no idea how to go about getting cloth, or how to start a fire for hot water. However, I am determined to figure it out. And quickly.

Okay, water. And... Of course, the water bucket is empty. I gather up the empty bucket and leave the house. Lifting the hem of my skirt, I run as fast as possible to the well in the town center. My feet skid to a stop, and I work vigorously to lower the bucket into the dark depths of the watery abyss. A distant splash noise tells me that my bucket has reached its destination, and I let out a relieved breath as I begin to raise it back up. This is taking much longer than I remembered when Rowan showed me. How deep is this well, anyway? Does it really need to be so damn deep? I grit my teeth in frustration as the seconds tick by.

When the bucket finally reaches the top of the well, I nearly cry in relief. Transferring the water into my bucket, I run back to the house, trying to keep the water from sloshing over the sides in my haste. I crash in through the door with wide eyes and fix my gaze on Rowan's chest to make sure he is still breathing. The slightest movement relieves my frantic mind, and I thank my lucky stars he is still alive. Although, how much longer that may be is anyone's guess. He looks as white as a corpse.

Lynet has already removed Rowan's clothes and has a blanket covering the bottom half of his body.

Okay, water, check. Next is fire.

A few glowing embers are still flickering in the charred wood from our last fire. Placing a few slivers of wood over the glowing remains, I blow on it lightly to stoke it into action. Nothing happens. Rowan makes it look so easy. As the seconds tick by, I begin to fear a flame will never catch. Finally, after several minutes and more than a few curse words, a shaving catches and blooms to life.

Pushing down the urge to jump up and down in excitement, I put on a few more thin pieces of kindling near the flame. The fire grows larger at an uncomfortably slow pace. I keep peering back, praying that everything will be alright. Rowan's chalky pallor does nothing to soothe my frantic mind.

Finally, the fire is large enough to heat the kettle of water.

All right now, cloth.

Looking around the room, I try to determine where to get extra cloth and remember my old clothing, which has been washed and folded in a pile near the bed. Walking to it, I rip off large strips and hand them to Lynet.

She changes the bloody compress on his shoulder with the cloth that I handed her.

Next, she lifts the blanket to tend to the wound on his leg. His skin is shredded, and a jagged mark runs the length of one calf. She binds the wound as tightly as she can, wrapping the ends of the cloth in a knot.

"Can you apply pressure to his shoulder? I must run to get more help."

She wipes the back of her hand over her cheek and leaves a smudge of blood across her cheek. Nodding my head, I place my hand over the already blood-soaked cloth and try not to heave up the contents of my stomach when he lets out a moan of pain.

Lynet leaves, and I am all alone with Rowan once again. I focus my attention on his face instead of the blood seeping out through the bandage beneath my hand. He can't leave me now.

Not when I just found him. My heart hurts just thinking of my life without him in it. How could this man be taken away when he is so full of life?

Although, I know that answer before the question has even left my mind. Life is not fair. Nothing about it is fair or makes sense. It is just a series of ongoing unfortunate actions that keep altering our lives over and over until our minds struggle to keep up with each new development. I smooth my hand over his chest and close my eyes as a tear trails down my cheek. At least he is still breathing. If he is still breathing, there is still hope. I cling to that hope like a drowning man to a raft. I will not give up on him. He didn't give up on me and I mean to repay the favor.

Lynet flings the door open, and trailing right behind her is Joy.

Joy kneels in front of me and stares into my eyes with an intensity that unnerves me.

"Anya," Joy says, taking me by the shoulders. "We need to stitch the wounds. It might be better if you weren't here for this."

"I want to... I can't...." My words are thick in my throat as I try to explain that I don't want to leave him. Not even for a moment. He saved me. Regardless of what he is or what shape he comes in. I care for him.

"It's all right," she says, hugging me. "You have done a wonderful job helping, but there will be a lot of blood, and we need to focus on Rowan."

She smooths my hair back and leads me to the door. If you want, you can wait at Lynet's house, and we can come get you just as soon as we are finished."

I know she is right about me leaving. If I stay and see all that blood.... smell all that blood, chances are I will be sick or worse, pass out, and I need them to focus on Rowan, not me. Taking a deep breath, I nod my head.

"But I am waiting outside. Right on the other side of the door."

"I understand." With that, she turns, and they begin mending his destroyed body.

Chapter 10.

When his screaming first starts, I vomit in the bushes. My body heaves as I empty the remnants of my breakfast onto a pile of soggy leaves. The vile liquid burns my throat, and I spit to get the taste of it out of my mouth. Grabbing a handful of snow, I swish it around my mouth before putting another handful on my fevered cheek. Never have I felt so powerless. With my head resting against the side of the house, I pray for his suffering to stop.

The agony in those screams is enough to make the strongest man quiver in fright as they echo through the forest. Several villagers pass by, glancing over with worried eyes and sympathetic words of encouragement. I barely hear them. All of my attention is focused on the door, waiting for Lynet to open it and tell me everything will be fine.

The screams finally stopped abruptly nearly an hour ago. Now, Rowan is quiet, and I press my ear against the door to see if there is any indication of what he is doing. I am pressed so tightly against the wood that when it is wrenched open, I fall straight into Lynet.

"Umph," she says, when I nearly topple us both.

"Anya, you can go in for a while and see him. We are done with the wound on his leg, but his shoulder still needs to be stitched.

Her hands are covered in his blood, and a mound of cloth lays next to the bed that is now deep crimson.

"Another wound to stitch? Will he be able to handle that? The screaming sounded so awful."

Joy and Lynet gave each other worried glances. Their strained expressions tell me everything I need to know.

"He has lost a lot of blood, Anya. And these types of injuries tend to become infected. Herbs will help, but nothing is guaranteed," Lynet says.

Lines of exhaustion are visible around her eyes, and she turns away to wash the blood off her hands.

"What happened in the woods?" Joy asks me.

"There were wolves. Four of them. They came out of nowhere, and I thought we would surely die. But then, Rowan. He changed."

I swallow a lump before continuing. Hopefully, his sisters already know about his transforming power and won't think I am insane when I tell them this. Hell. Maybe I am insane. Perhaps I imagined the entire thing and will sound like a raving lunatic when I try to explain it to them. "He changed into a wolf and killed them. He saved me."

They don't look surprised. They don't flinch or question my words. Joy nods and places the back of her hand on her brother's forehead.

"You know?" I ask.

"Yes," Joy replies. "We know."

"But how...?"

"He should tell you the rest himself," Lynet says before I finish this line of inquiry.

How is it possible that a flesh and blood-man can transform so quickly into a beast? And what else don't I know about him? Perhaps they can all change similarly, and I am the silly outsider who stumbles across their little secret.

For now, I wrestle down my growing unease and quiet the questions in my head. After he is out of danger, I will get my answers, but for now, I focus on what must be done to keep him alive and comfortable.

Unable to stay away from him any longer, I kneel beside his bed and place my hand in his. There is no returning pressure as I squeeze his hand, nor did I expect one. His skin looks white as snow, and his breathing is shallow.

"What can I do to help?" I ask as a tear makes its way down my cheek. "There must be something I can do."

"Can you go to Old Man Duncan's house and bring back a pint of his whiskey?" Lynet asks me. "It will help dull the pain if he wakes again and also to sanitize the wound."

I kiss his hand before whispering into his ear. "You can't die when I have only just found you. Please, Rowan. I need you here with me."

A slight squeeze from his fingers puts my mind to ease, but that small movement may have also been my imagination. I pray it is the former. I leave the house and make my way to Duncan's house. It is set back from the town, further into the forest than any other of the houses. His house is also built on the ground instead of in the trees. Rowan had joked he would have fallen and broken his neck by now if he had to traverse those bridges after sampling his whiskey so often.

Dusk has begun to take hold, and the last rays of the sun are disappearing under the horizon. Long shadows crisscross the path before me, and I shiver in cold and shock as I make my way forward.

There are no lights inside Duncan's house, and the forest is eerily quiet as I finally reach my destination. I give the door three loud raps, but no one stirs inside. I lift my hand to knock again but pause when footsteps come from within. A moment later, the door is wrenched open, and Duncan stands on the threshold.

Completely. Naked.

My eyes drift down to the exposed flesh below his waist, but I immediately snap my gaze onto his face. Nope. Not something I care to see at this moment. Or any moment for that matter.

Duncan has a liquor bottle in one hand and the other hand he uses to reach down and scratch himself between his thighs. The scratching continues for some time, and I must clear my throat to interrupt his ministrations. He closes one eye, and only then does he focus on my face, scrunching up his face as if trying to place where he knows me from.

"Anya! What on earth are you doing here so late? I was just having a visit from the widow Brackenhurst." He leans in and whispers, "Her husband died a few years back, and she needs someone to keep her warm these cold winter nights."

His laughter shakes his big belly. It shakes everything, actually, and I deliberately focus my attention on his face to prevent it from traveling elsewhere.

At that moment, an older woman in a long grey dress and a mass of black curls squeezes past Duncan before scampering down the dirt path.

"Ah, don't be like that, love. Not even a kiss goodbye?" he asks.

She turns around, and her ruddy cheeks are pulled into a smile.

"Maybe if you are lucky, tomorrow night I'll let you kiss me goodbye," she says before winking and continuing down the street with a little swing in her hips.

"Oh, that woman. She is a spirited lass if ever there was one."

I shake my head to rid myself of this increasingly disturbing exchange. "I'm sorry to disturb your, um... evening. But Lynet asked me to come for a pint of whiskey. Rowan is hurt, and she needs it to help calm him and disinfect the wound."

He sobers up remarkably quick and sucks in a breath. "Hurt, you say? Well, we better get you back on your way then. I hope it wasn't bad."

"It is indeed," I reply grimly.

He walks into his house and returns moments later with a pint of whiskey. "I'll wish the best for the lad."

He squeezes me in a tight hug before handing me the liquor. The embrace takes me by surprise. More from the emotion that overcomes me than the fact that a naked man is pressed up against my body.

"Me too, Duncan. Thank you."

When I return to the house, Rowan is awake and moaning on the bed. His eyes lock onto mine, imploring me to help him. I hand the bottle to Lynet, and she pours some into a cup.

Leaning his head forward, she gets a few sips into his mouth before he refuses any more.

"Anya," Joy says, "we are going to sew up the arm now if you want to wait outside again."

Rowan's eyes flash to me and his pained expression grips my heart.

"I am going to stay." I walk to the bottle of whiskey and down an enormous gulp, thankfully without choking. It burns like fire in my throat before sitting comfortably in the pit of my stomach. I kneel beside the bed and put a hand on Rowan's cheek.

"I'm going to stay," I say again to reassure him.

He seems to relax, and the fire liquid gives me the strength to block out the smell and sight of the blood.

I focus on the amber flecks in his eyes and the crinkles at the corners of his eyes. I stroke a hand across his forehead, and he squeezes my other hand every time the needle pierces his skin.

"More whiskey," he chokes out. I place the cup to his lips, and he swallows nearly half before they resume. He doesn't cry out in pain, but his teeth are clenched together so hard I'm surprised they don't crack.

Joy is the one stitching, and she needs to wipe her hand after each stitch to remove the blood on her hands so she can grasp the needle. Her hands are remarkably steady. Other than a few twitches in her eye, she is utterly unwavering in her work. When the last stitch is finally done, I breathe a sigh of relief, thinking the hard part is over.

I am wrong.

When Lynet pours whiskey over the wound, Rowan's scream is heartbreaking. His back bows off the bed, and the cords in his neck look like they might snap.

"I'm sorry, Rowan," Lynet tells him. "It's done now."

He lays back down, trembling uncontrollably, and his muscles twitch with shock and adrenaline. The women wrap the wound expertly and clean up the area around the bed while I run my fingers through his hair.

"Thank you for staying," he whispers.

"You didn't leave me," I tell him with a crooked smile. "I'm not leaving you."

"The bleeding has slowed significantly," Lynet says, peeking under the bandages. "If you get water and broth into him, he should regain his strength quickly."

"Really? He will recover?" I was afraid to ask the question, but now that I have, I hold my breath and wait for the answer.

"You aren't getting rid of me that easy, Little Bird," he jokes.

Lynet and Joy pack up their things to leave, but Lynet puts a pouch full of herbs in my hand.

"Make him tea with these herbs every four hours, and be sure he drinks all of it. That will help with preventing infection. That is what we need to fear going forward."

I notice she doesn't directly answer my question, but the fact that they don't seem alarmed enough to stay is a good sign.

"I will be back in the morning to change his bandages and check for fever," Lynet says.

She gives me a fierce embrace, and her body is trembling nearly as much as mine from leftover adrenaline. I assume that is why she had to get Joy for the stitching. Joy's hands are as eerily still while she packs up the rest of her things and places them in the basket. Her steadfast movements are a bit disconcerting after what she just had to do, but the weariness in her eyes tells me she isn't completely unaffected.

When they exit the house, she throws one more look back at her brother with worried eyes that are heavy with exhaustion.

I have no idea what to do for him now other than Lynet's instructions. So, I don't move from my spot next to the bed except to add wood to the fire when it begins to die down. I lay my head on the pillow beside his but refuse to close my eyes.

What if they are wrong, and he dies while I am asleep?

The thought keeps me awake the entire night even though Rowan falls into a deep restless sleep. My eyes ache with fatigue, but no matter how often I try to sleep, it never comes. The night stretches before me like a never-ending void of uncertainty that my mind refuses to dismiss. Questions circle my mind interrupted only by the blinding realization that Rowan is a shape-shifting wolf. My wolf. I can't focus on my current feelings. The emotions keep slipping through my mind like sand with no grain taking root.

I try to sort the thoughts one at a time. Am I afraid of him? No. Do I understand it? Also no. But do I care for him? Absolutely. And I want him to live. I want to stay by his side as long as he will have me and tend to these wounds until the danger has passed. Perhaps even longer.

When the sun begins to peek through the window, I lift my weary body off the floor and walk to the fireplace, stoking the dying embers back to life. I have become somewhat proficient in tending to a fire in such a short time, and a small bubble of pride rises in my chest. At least I can do this much for him.

Grabbing the bag of herbs Lynet gave me, I pour some into a cup and top it with hot water from the kettle. I add a scoop of honey and bring it to the bed.

"Rowan, your tea," I whisper.

He doesn't wake, and I try again to rouse him with the same effect.

His ashy complexion suddenly looks like I am staring at a corpse, and I can't see his chest rising and falling.

"Rowan!" I yell and shake his body roughly, sloshing the tea onto the floor.

"Ugh, good lord, woman, that hurt," he says, cracking an eye. I realize my fingers are digging into his bandaged arm and quickly let go.

I let out a long breath and became dizzy with relief. "I couldn't wake you for your tea," I tell him, holding the now half-empty mug.

Propping himself into a semi-sitting position, he licks his dry lips and reaches for the cup. He drinks the remaining tea in three long gulps.

"Thirsty?" I ask.

"Yes. Can I get some water also? My mouth is so dry, I feel like I've eaten sand."

"Of course." I hurry to the bucket, returning moments later with water. "You must be dehydrated. You lost a lot of blood."

So much blood. The memory returns to me, and even now, the coppery tang lingers in the air. A shiver runs through me at the memory of it soaking through his bandages. I close my eyes and breathe through my mouth to quiet my rolling stomach. It's no use. The memory of it is etched into my brain.

Fuck it. I walk to the other side of the room, and take a swig of the liquor, which doesn't taste nearly as bad as it used to. Now, it seems more like a comfort since I know it will settle my jittery stomach. Besides, it will also give me the strength for the impending conversation. And there will definitely be a conversation.

Straightening my back, I turn around to see Rowan sitting fully upright now, staring at me with an amused expression, even though he is pale as a ghost.

"What?" I ask with raised eyebrows.

"Oh, nothing. Just glad to see you getting acquainted with old man Duncan's whiskey. Seems you have a real taste for it."

I contemplate throwing the bottle at him but decide he can't handle another injury right now, so I place it back on the table and take a deep breath. Control. Remember your control. He owes me an explanation for whatever happened in the woods, and getting angry won't help get me the answers to my questions.

"It's the blood. I can't stand the smell or sight of it. I never could."

"Well, in that case, you may need another swig before we change these bandages," he said with a lopsided grin.

"Oh no. Your sister said she would be back to change those. I don't know if I would be much help passed out on the floor after I faint at the sight."

But the whiskey is loosening my muscles and settling my stomach. The thought of the blood fades into the back of my mind instead of a sharp reminder laced with anxiety. Now, it is mostly an afterthought. It is a mild worry that floats between thoughts.

The liquor dulls my worry, and I take one more drink for good measure before kneeling next to the bed.

I open my mouth to speak, but he cuts me off with a hand on my cheek. "Thank you for staying," he says, running his thumb over my lips. "It made the pain more bearable with you here beside me."

Oh lord. How was I supposed to be angry with him now? In truth, I have never been angry with him. Only scared and frustrated. And if I'm being honest, I am hurt. My time here with him has been the best of my life. I felt like I could finally begin to believe in something. Believe in someone. And now this. The omission feels like a chasm in the life I began to hope for.

"You stayed by me when I was sick. I was only returning the favor."

"I don't believe you," he says. That damn thumb strokes lazy circles across my jaw. "I think you stayed because you wanted to. I think you stay because you care about me."

The last few weeks flash through my memory. Every touch. Every lopsided grin. Every second of our time together. I do care about him, which terrifies and excites me in equal measure. Do I dare to hope this might be the future I often dreamed of?

He is seeping into every secret resolve and breaking down my barriers. Perhaps if I just... Leaning up, I hover before him, brushing back a strand of hair from his forehead.

"Rowan..." I say, his breath mingling with my own. I prepare to declare that I do care about him. More than he could ever know. The heat of his hand on my cheek encourages me to move forward when suddenly his amber eyes take on a darker hue and remind me of the brown eyes of my wolf.

Reality slams into me like a boulder, and I remember exactly what I wanted to discuss before I got distracted by those damn expressive eyes.

"Wait a minute," I say, holding up my hand. "You owe me an explanation before this goes any further. What in the actual hell happened in those woods?"

"So, my plans to distract you with my wily charm have been unsuccessful?" he says, wiggling his eyebrows.

I swat him with the back of my hand, remembering belatedly he is injured, and hit him directly on his bandaged shoulder.

"Oh, I'm sorry," I say as more blood begins to seep out through the bandage. He groans and leans back against the wall.

"I suppose I deserved that one," he moans.

I try to place another cloth over the top, but it is useless. The bandage will need to be changed now.

Sighing, I pick up a new stack of cloth from the floor and place it on his lap. "Well, I guess we are changing these bandages after all. But you need to talk to me to distract me while I am doing this. And by talk, I mean I want an explanation," I say with one raised eyebrow.

He sighs but doesn't argue while I begin unwinding the linen cloth from around his shoulder.

"I don't want you to leave," he tells me. Those large amber eyes plead with me to understand.

"Then be honest with me, Rowan. All I want is the truth."

I'm afraid of whatever he is about to tell me, but I'm more afraid of not knowing. I have been left in the dark long enough. Kept locked away and out of sight. I want to live, and sometimes living hurts. I'm ready to hear the truth.

Rowan closes his eyes and leans his head against the wall again as I tend to his wound.

"Magda is my mother," he says quietly before laying his head back on the pillow, as if the words have caused him more pain than the injuries he sustained.

Chapter 11.

My hands pause with the bandage in midair. I must have misheard him. That can't be. It doesn't make sense.

He opens his eyes and turns to look at me with a haunted expression. His usual humor is absent. No laughter crinkling around his eyes. No smirk lifting the corner of his lips. Just pain etched around the lines of his face.

"My mother was once a healer. She lived here with my father for many years and was loved and respected by everyone. Right after I was born, a sickness swept through the town and claimed my father in its passage. She was never the same after that."

My fingers begin moving again, wrapping the cloth around his shoulder even though a strange humming has begun in my head.

"She became consumed with the need to control anything within her reach. This obsession spilled over into the art of black magic. Your mother heard of her growing power and lured her to the castle with promises of wealth and influence. My mother wanted neither of those things, but she did want what that sort of connection could buy. Knowledge and supplies. She practiced day and night, driven to find what she had yet to obtain. The key to resurrection and immortality. Death defined her craft until she practiced on anything and everything within her reach, including her children."

I pull the ends of the bandage together, tying them in place so they don't come undone. I am so focused on Rowan's words that his blood barely registers in my mind. Everything else just fades into the background as he speaks. I have so many questions, but my throat is thick with emotion.

Out of all the things I expected him to say, this is not it. I thought perhaps the mushrooms had some sort of long-term hallucinogenic response. Or that long-term trauma altered my reality into something twisted and unreal. But this. This is too real. Too close to my past. I close my eyes and focus my breathing before asking my first question.

"So, you were the wolf outside my bedroom? For all those years?"

"You have known me for much longer than just these past weeks, Anya. And I have known you. If in perhaps a slightly different form."

I remember my tiny body, crying with fear and anger, all alone in my cell. I remember the feeling of his warm tongue licking the tips of my fingers, and cherishing this connection to the outside world. A lone wolf became my unlikely companion in that isolated environment.

Something about his story doesn't make sense, though. Other than the fact that he can change into a wolf, of course.

"But Magda. She is so old. She must be close to eighty or even ninety years old if looks are any indication. She can't possibly be your mother."

"The power consumes her. Not only her mind but also her body. Every time she calls upon the realm of the undead, she trades something of herself in return. Little by little, her life is pulled away until all that remains of her is a haggard old woman who would do anything to find the answers she seeks."

"So, it is just two women obsessed with finding the key to immortality and reuniting with their lost lovers," I say.

It is pretty romantic if you take away the bat-shit-crazy aspect of the entire situation. Two women so desperate to be reunited with their long-dead lovers they would do anything to have one last chance at a reunion.

"Two women?" Rowan asks. "Your mother has lost someone also?"

With a resigned sigh, I tell him about my father. "My mother was only fourteen when she met my father, Benjamin. From what I have pieced together over the years, he was a servant at her family's estate. What started as an innocent childhood friendship quickly turned into something more. They fell desperately in love in the following years, and she soon found herself pregnant with his child."

"You?"

"Yes. Me. When it was found out by her parents, Benjamin was torn limb from limb, and his remains were fed to the swine as punishment for having dared touch their daughter. They sent Elizabeth off to give birth in secret and she kept me hidden away for the first few years of my life. Elizabeth was married off to her husband, and I came to live with her at the castle after it was determined they would bear no other children."

"In the dungeon?"

"Not right away. At first, I lived in the nursery with several other girls, but the older I grew, the more apparent my appearance resembled my father's. Her husband was consumed with jealousy at the thought of another man having touched his wife. He said the only way he would allow me to live was if I stayed out of sight. In the dungeon."

Even the memory of that horrible place sends a shiver up my spine.

Rowan rubs the back of my hand with his thumb and brings it to his lips to kiss.

"Anya, Look at me. You don't have to ever go back there. Not if I have anything to say about it. You can stay here with us. Stay here with me." His eyes are imploring me to say yes, and it is on the tip of my tongue to agree. I want to say, Yes, Rowan, I will stay. The words are stuck in my throat, and I settle for leaning up to brush my lips against his. When I open my mouth to say something, a knock on the door interrupts our conversation.

Lynet walks in, followed by two burly men. The men are so tall they have trouble fitting through the front door and must bend down so their heads don't hit the top of the door frame. Both carry large buckets filled with steaming hot water.

"Well, it's nice to see you are awake," she says, kneeling before Rowan. She places a hand on his forehead and smiles approvingly when her hand meets cool flesh. "No fever. That's a good sign."

"He drank all of his tea," I supply.

"Good. You have been incredibly helpful," Lynet tells me before pulling me into a quick hug. "Now, to change these bandages."

"I already changed them."

Her eyebrows shoot up in surprise and she turns to check my handiwork with a chuckle. "Well, so you did."

The two men behind her place the buckets next to the water and back away to the door slowly. It looks like they are afraid they might be asked to assist with caring for an injured man, and the thought is about as appealing as peeling their nails off with pliers.

"Anything else you need, love?" The larger man asks.

"No, Arthur. Thank you for carrying the water for me."

So, this is her husband. I hadn't pictured her with someone so rugged but watching him lean down and kiss her, I can see they fit together seamlessly.

"That's no problem," her husband replies. "You know you shouldn't be doing anything too strenuous in your condition." He gives her a wink before they exit and close the door behind them.

"Delicate state?" Rowan asks, looking bemused. "Good lord, Lynet. You aren't with a child again, are you? You could already amass a small army with the brood you have."

"Oh, you just mind your business," she says, swatting him with the back of her hand. "Every child is a blessing and will be treated as such."

She mumbles under her breath, "If only Arthur could keep his hands off me for five bloody minutes."

A bubble of laughter rises, and it erupts from my lips before I can cover my mouth. "Congratulations on the baby," I tell her, trying to stifle my laugh.

"Thank you, Anya. Now, on to the task at hand. A bath."

The look of horror on Rowan's face does not escape Lynet's attention.

"You don't mean to bathe me like one of your children, now do you? Would you like to swaddle me in a nappy as well?”

"Well, how else will we get all that blood and dirt off you? And look at the state of your bed. Covered in dried blood. No. This won't do."

"Anya. Can you help him stand while I change the covering on the bed, please?"

"Of course." Bending down, I hook his arm around my neck, and with much effort and more than a few grunts, we manage to get him into a standing position.

By the time Lynet has the bed cleaned, Rowan has sweat dripping down his face and is trembling with the effort it takes to remain standing.

"All better," she says, wadding the soiled linen into a ball and putting it into her basket.

When I lower him back onto the bed, he pulls me down with him, so I am laying on top of him. His cheek is pressed to mine, and his skin is damp with exertion.

"Stay still for a minute, Little Bird," he whispers in my ear. My position on top of him is awkward, and Lynet's gazes at me with humor as I attempt to extricate myself from his grasp after a few minutes. His breathing has returned to normal, and the sickly pale complexion from over-taxing his injured body has begun to return to normal.

"Well, that was a bit more of a task than I imagined," Lynet says. "Perhaps we should hold off on the bath for another day."

"I can do it once he has settled a bit."

"Are you sure?" she asks, raising her eyebrows. I know she doesn't mean to offend me by the question. She is likely referring to my visceral reaction to the sight of the blood.

"Yes. I can manage."

"Well, all right then. I'll leave you to it." She places another pouch of herbs in my hand. This one is much larger than the last one. "This should last for several days. I will be back tomorrow to check on him, but please don't hesitate to fetch me if he develops a fever or if you have any cause for concern."

"I will."

She nods and gives her brother one more glance before exiting the house.

"She is worried about you."

"She is always worried about me," he says with the hint of a smile. "She has been my mother for most of my life and can't help herself."

"Why don't you rest a bit. I will keep these buckets hot for a bath when you are ready," I say, smoothing my hand over his cheek.

The sight of him trembling and pale only moments ago has me more concerned than I let on. He lost too much blood. At what point does the human body simply give up instead of trying to restore the vital fluid that it needs to sustain life? I refuse to dwell on that thought. Instead, I pull the blanket around his shoulders and bring the buckets to the fireplace, setting them just outside the embers. They should stay plenty warm there. When I turn around, Rowan is already fast asleep.

Chapter 12.

The water is the perfect temperature when I pull it away from the fireplace. I set both buckets beside the bed and peer into the clear liquid. My reflection looks back at me, and the image transports me back to my life in the dungeon.

How many times have I looked into a similar bucket of water over the years and seen sad, lifeless eyes staring back at me?

This reflection is different though. I can't place my finger on what the difference is at first, but after a few moments, I realize what it is. A spark. My eyes no longer look haunted and empty but full of something almost indefinable. A flame that resides not only in my eyes but behind every cell of my body. I can feel it beneath my skin. Burning beneath the surface of my body. What I see is hope. I want to live. I want to grasp my future with both hands and rip it wide open to see what awaits me. But mostly, I want to love.

I look at Rowan, who is still sleeping soundly. I want to love this man and let him love me. Something shifts inside me as I stare at this beautiful, broken man. All my fear melts away. My fear of hope diminishes into something that is no longer the main plot of my story but is simply a subline in the distant recess of my life. My fear cannot control me any longer if I want to break free of my mother's fantom grasp. It is at that moment I realize, yes. I want to stay. I want to hope and embrace whatever the future has to offer. My fear will no longer hold me prisoner like the scared girl in that cell. This is my life, and I intend to control it.

I brush a stray lock of hair off Rowan's forehead, and his eyes flutter open.

"Ready to get washed up, sleepy head?"

"How long was I asleep?" he asks, arching his back like a cat.

"Most of the day. I didn't want to wake you and thought you could use all the rest you could get."

"Mmm," he says, propping himself up on his elbow.

I hand him a cup of tea, which he drinks greedily before swiping the back of his hand across his mouth to catch a few stray droplets running down his chin.

"Bath time?" He wiggles his eyebrows suggestively, and I laugh.

“You are incorrigible. Halfway to your death bed, you still have a sense of humor."

"What else do we have to live for if not humor and love?" he asks with a lopsided grin.

Damn that grin. And what did he mean by love? Yup, I'm definitely overthinking that one.

Trying to control my wayward thoughts, I tear my gaze away and clear my throat.

"If you would prefer not to wash me," he says with a pout, "I'm sure Lynet would be able to, but I must say, I would definitely prefer if you did it."

"I don't mind," I say, trying to keep my voice from quivering.

I can do this. Calming my racing heart, I dip the washcloth in the bucket and squeeze out the excess water. Rowan is leaning back with his eyes closed now, and the lack of his scrutiny gives me the strength I need to continue. I peel back the edge of the blanket, and to my intense disappointment, a layer of clothing separates me from his body. I mean, his injuries.

"We must remove these if I am to clean you properly."

"By all means, take them off then." I can tell he is holding back a grin, and it causes my spine to straighten. Well, it can't all be fun and games now, can it? Someone has to take this seriously. Even if my traitorous thighs are quivering at the thought of his bare skin under my hands. I am determined to get him cleaned and his wounds rebandaged. A few spots of blood are already seeping through the bandages I applied. Although the bleeding has slowed significantly, it will take time before it subsides completely.

"Lift your hips," I order him.

"I'm not so sure about that," he says. His grin is replaced with an uncharacteristically serious expression.

"And why not?"

"Because I don't have anything on under these pants."

I pull back, and a soft, oh, leaves my mouth. The images that spring to my mind do nothing to quell this burning ache in my stomach. Instead, I deflect. "All right, the shirt then."

"Better choice, Little Bird."

He moves into a sitting position, and I tug the hem of his shirt up until it clears his broad shoulders. I toss the shirt onto the end of the bed and count to ten before continuing. Control. Remember your control. But the sight of him bare-chested is more than I anticipated. I'm having trouble counting the last few numbers as I stare at his finely sculpted chest and the trail of hair that begins at his stomach and ends somewhere beneath the waistband of his pants.

Snapping my attention back to his face, I notice he doesn't look amused. His expression is so serious I'm afraid I may have insulted him by perusing the landscape of his body. That is until I see the bulge in his pants and realize he is just as affected by me as I am by him.

"I must say," he begins. "It is rather impressive that I can barely stand, but I am so attracted to you that you can still have such a visceral reaction on me."

"Me?"

"Yes, Anya. I have never seen a creature as beautiful as you. Nor met another with such a fierce desire to live life to its fullest. I wish I could see life through your eyes. You make everything seem so new and exciting."

"It is new and exciting. Did you forget I spent most of my life in a dungeon?" I ask with a half-smile. "This town. And you. Everything is so wonderful."

"Are you saying you care for me, Anya?"

"Care is too light a word," I say before thinking.

He reaches out and tucks a strand behind my ear. "I agree."

My hand reaches up and runs along the tight muscles of his body before skimming the waistband of his pants.

I lean forward and press my lips to his.

His response is tentative at first but becomes more insistent with each passing second. His uninjured arm reaches up to graze the fabric just beneath my breast, and I let out a shudder of pleasure. Every sensation makes me feel so alive with passion and bravery. My skin practically hums with energy as he sucks on my bottom lip and runs his tongue over mine again and again. This feeling is something I wouldn't exchange for all the riches in the world. It is an all-consuming force all on its own, and I absorb every second of it while it lasts.

Unfortunately, all good things must come to an end, and I pull back. I rest my forehead on his while our ragged breathing returns to normal.

"You may kill me yet," he laughs.

"Me? You are the one who started it with..." I point towards the bulge in his trousers.

"I can't be to blame. He has a mind of his own."

I laugh at his lewd remark. No one has ever talked to me so unobstructed, and I absolutely love it.

"Well, tell "him" to behave so we can finish this bath and get you back to bed. Too much excitement can't be good for you just now."

Rowan lays back on the bed with a sigh. "Down, boy. We need to behave ourselves."

I stifle back another laugh as I bring the washcloth to his chest to wipe away any signs of his bloody ordeal. As I make the first pass across his skin and see the beads of water glistening on his chest, I know I am in trouble. My fingers itch to touch the stray droplets nested among the hair at the waist of his pants. I dip the cloth into the second bucket to rinse it off.

After several more passes, his chest is finally free of any dirt or dried blood, but I can't help myself and squeeze out the cloth onto his stomach one last time. He sucks in a breath, and the action causes his stomach to suck in. Water pools in his belly button, and a few drops leak down the sides of his stomach. One tiny part of me wants to lean down and lick that water from his stomach, but another rational part tells me to keep my mind on the task at hand. Stupid rational brain.

"All right. Time for the pants to come off."

He lets out a groan. "You are killing me with that language."

"Get your mind out of the gutter." Yes, I am a total hypocrite.

It takes a few moments of lifting and grunting before his pants are entirely removed. And just as he promised earlier, he has absolutely nothing underneath. A fierce blush begins up my cheeks and runs down my neck until I'm pretty sure that even my toes have turned crimson.

"Would you prefer that I cover up?"

As much as I want to say no, and I really want to say no, I will never accomplish anything while staring at that exposed part of him between his thighs, no matter how impressive that exposed part is. I have seen enough naked men strapped to my mother's bed to know that what he has below the waist far exceeds normal standards. I have even seen couples procreating in the hallways of my mother's castle, some of them willingly, some of them not. However, what I witnessed in that castle will be nothing like what happens between

Rowan and me when we eventually come together.

"You better stop staring at me like that, Little Bird, or no amount of blood loss will keep him from waking."

Even as he says the words, his shaft twitches and begins to swell. Oh lord, how easy it would be to just reach out and stroke it. Is it as velvety soft as it looks? But then my eyes stray to the bandage on his leg that blood is already beginning to seep through, and I sigh.

Let the injured man heal and control these wayward impulses? Or throw my leg over his body and feel what the hardening erection feels like between my thighs? Decisions, decisions.

I swing my eyes away and focus my resolve to keep my mind out of the gutter.

How hard can that be?

I hand him a towel, and he places it over his lap, but the mischievous glimmer remains in his eyes.

I can't tell if he is enjoying my discomfort or me bathing him, the urge to pinch him. I refrain from further injuring him, however, and continue my task until every inch of him is clean. Well, almost every inch.

Once that is done, I change his bandages. I'm relieved they appear to be healing well and that there is no sign of oozing or swelling around the injuries. The tea seems to be doing its job.

Once he is redressed, I take the buckets outside and empty them behind the house. On the way back inside, I catch the smell of my own pungent aroma and realize I could also use a good wash. So, I take the buckets back to the well and fill them one at a time. I see several people on my two trips back and forth, most of whom I recognize now.

This town is beginning to feel comfortable, and dare I say, like home. I love the smell of wood smoke floating lazily in the air and the children running across the bridges above me. This place is truly a remarkable haven, and I feel fortunate to be a part of their small community.

After I return and the buckets have reached a deliciously warm temperature, I place them on the table. Rowan has fallen asleep and is snoring softly in his bed. Glancing at him once more to be sure he is sleeping, I take my dress off to wash.

There is no separate area to conceal myself, but I don't care. Standing in the middle of his home with nothing on is exhilarating. However, I do shutter the windows first. There is no need for little children to poke their heads through and get an eyeful of my nudity.

The water feels so good on my bare skin, and I sigh as it trickles down my neck and chest. My nipples pebble at the contrast of the warm water against my cool skin, and goosebumps break out across my skin. I let the cloth glide over my skin, cleaning and warming me in slow, languid movements. A sharp intake of breath behind me causes me to pause mid-wipe. I am turned away from him but can feel his eyes on me.

"Do you want me to look away?" Rowan asks with a voice husky with sleep. "If you want me to, I will. But God help me, Anya, I don't want to."

I think about it for only a moment before shaking my head.

"I like your eyes on me."

Then, I do something that makes me feel brave and lightheaded. I turn around. His eyes are burning with desire. They sweep up and down the length of my body, drinking in every detail of me like a man who has been to sea for months and finally sees land. He looks at me like I am his salvation.

And I fucking love it.

Taking a deep breath, I drag the cloth up and down my body, and his eyes track the movement of my hand.

"You are temptation in its purest form," he groans.

"It's only fair. I got to see all of you. Now you get to see all of me."

"It is taking all of my willpower not to get off this bed and come touch every delicious curve of yours."

The ache in my stomach becomes an inferno, and I can feel the dampness collect between my legs. Even though my legs tremble with the need to go to him, I stand in one spot, finishing what I started before dropping the washcloth back into the bucket with a splash.

He had better hurry up and heal. I don't want to be the one responsible for tearing open those stitches. Joy may not be impressed if I explain why she must stitch her brother back up.

Time.

All we need is time. And an arsenal of willpower.

Chapter 13.

Over the next two weeks, Rowan's injuries begin to heal, and his strength returns, slowly but surely. I sit on the bed next to him most nights with the fire crackling in the fireplace.

He reads several of his books and traces his progress on the page.

I follow along, picking up new words as he reads. My embarrassment at being illiterate begins to recede a little more each day, and I take pride in my ability to learn quickly. He is a patient teacher who doesn't criticize or rebuke me when I get a word wrong or can't figure out the pronunciation.

Tonight, he is stroking the back of my arm, and my eyes close while I soak in the feeling of contentment that wraps around me like a blanket. I have been careful to avoid any more intimate moments to prevent the inevitable injuries that would surely follow. However, each day, his wounds will be fully healed, and I look forward to the time when we can finally act on our desire.

"Tell me something about yourself," I say, wanting to know more about this man who is still a bit of a mystery. He has told me bits and pieces of his life but has yet to delve into more detail about his family or growing up without a mother. I wonder if he is trying to hide something or just reluctant to bring up such things again.

"That sickness I had as a boy. The one that almost killed me…"

"Yes?" I say, remembering our earlier discussion.

"It wasn't just a sickness. No child wants to believe their mother would intentionally hurt them. But on the third day of my sickness, I began to question the medicine Magda was giving me. I was perfectly healthy before she began giving it to me, and in just a few short days, I was too sick to stand."

I hold my breath as he tells me his story. Winding my fingers through his, I squeeze to show my support as he continues.

"My body kept rejecting it. Each day, I threw it up, and each day, she made me drink it again. The last day. After six days of heaving and vomiting, my body finally absorbed the damnable poison."

His jaw flexes as he remembers back to that awful day.

I reach up and run a finger along his jaw, feeling the muscles flex under my touch.

"She used me. She made me her first experiment before moving on to bigger prey. She knew I was too little to fight her off and used that to her advantage. And now I must live with the consequences for the rest of my life."

"How old were you?"

"Eight."

"I'm sorry that happened to you. I'm sorry you were used and discarded the same way my mother used me. Childhood should be full of laughter and mischief. Not worrying about if you can trust the people who are supposed to keep you safe above all else."

We fall back into a comfortable silence. Both of us lost in the memory of that misplaced trust.

My eyes drift closed as his fingers dance up and down my arm and his movements lull me into peaceful tranquility. His fingers cease stroking, and he tilts his head, straining to hear some phantom sound.

It takes me a moment, but I pick up a few murmurs as well. At first they are faint but become louder as the seconds go on. All at once, a loud cheer goes up in the village, and we scramble to our feet to see what the commotion is about.

Gathering our cloaks, we step outside into the chilly night air.

People are lined up along the trail leading into town. Groups of men walk past them, accepting claps on their backs and handshakes from the eager observers. The men clearly need a bath, with dirt-streaked faces and soiled clothing, but that doesn't diminish the broad smiles on each man's face.

Lynet's husband, Arthur, and Joy's husband, Simon, are among the hunters. Arthur gives us a wink as he walks by with a grin stretching from ear to ear. As they travel past, the reason for their jovial mood becomes obvious.

The men work in groups of two to carry large poles hoisted on their shoulders. Each pole has an impressively large animal tied up by its feet, causing the poles to bend precariously under the weight. As they pass by Rowan's house, I count five animals. Two elk and two deer are at the head of the procession. Then comes a massive wild boar, strung up by its hind legs. Its white tusks glint in the moonlight, razor sharp and dripping with blood.

"You know what this means, Little Bird?" Rowan whispers in my ear, his smile stretching from ear to ear.

"What?"

"Tonight, we feast. A celebration always follows such a bountiful harvest."

My mouth salivates at the thought of eating Lynet's beef stew again. I have discovered these last few weeks that the town has plenty of bread and vegetables, but meat is often scarce. The animals have migrated further down the mountain to escape the colder weather, and traveling longer distances for bigger prey is necessary. Rabbits and the occasional bobcat can only go so far, and fresh meat is a real treat in the winter.

"Another celebration? So soon after the last one?"

"Oh, yes. If there is one thing this village loves to do, it is celebrate," he says with a grin.

"Hold on." Rowan rushes back into the house and returns a few seconds later, holding a bundle in his hands.

"What is that?"

He unwraps the cloth and I let out a shudder of disgust at the sight of the dried mushrooms.

"Don't worry, Love. These are Morel mushrooms and are not poisonous. I promise you. Everyone brings something to the celebration, and I have more mushrooms than I can eat this year. Will you try them?"

I am stuck on the fact that he called me Love and that it sent a tiny thrill up my back.

Wanting to be brave, I nod, willing the fear out of my mind. But if I get sick from these damn things again, I will be supremely angry at him for talking me into this.

He pulls on my hand, and we follow the rest of the town into the circle where the last celebration took place. The townspeople make quick work of the preparations. They are assembling makeshift tables and setting a large bonfire alight. Dozens of cauldrons are placed around the fire, and everyone adds something to the pots until each one is brimming to the top with delicious-smelling broth and thick chunks of red meat. The hunters stand off to one side, preparing the animals and harvesting every scrap of meat from the bones. The bones and hides are set aside to be utilized the following day.

Rowan explains the uses for each, ranging from broth, fertilizer, instruments, clothing, and medicine. It is truly remarkable how I went from knowing so little about the world to soaking up this vast amount of knowledge in such a short time.

I thirst for more knowledge and eagerly absorb every detail.

Rowan grabs two cups from a nearby table and fills them to the brim with red liquid. When he hands me the cup, I smell it. Instead of the sour smell of Duncan's whiskey, this liquid smells sweet, like berries and honey.

When I take the first sip, I moan a bit too loud. Two women turn towards me with wide eyes before bursting into laughter. My cheeks flame red, and I look at Rowan, who is grinning also.

"Keep making noises like that, Anya, and you'll be in trouble before this night is through."

I quirk an eyebrow at him. "You say that like it's a bad thing."

His hungry gaze drops to my mouth.

I bite my bottom lip before taking another sip of my wine. A trickle of the sweet liquid drips down my chin, and he leans forward to wipe it away with the pad of his thumb. Bringing his thumb to his mouth, he licks the wine off with a slow, delicious caress of his tongue, all the while keeping his eyes on mine.

Holy hell, is that hot.

I swallow the thick lump that has formed in my throat and force myself to look away before the heat between my thighs burst into flames. This man is dangerous in all the right ways.

The pots of stew are beginning to boil, and the scents wafting through the air can only be described as heavenly. A group of older children start ladling the stew into bowls and passing them around the circle. One of the bowls is offered to Rowan and me, and he takes it gratefully. We take turns eating the decadent stew, and Rowan is right. The mushrooms are delicious, just as he predicted.

The mixture of wine and stew causes my face to flush, and my smile comes more easily as the night wears on.

A woman I have never met grabs my hand and pulls me into a circle where all the village's women grasp hands and twirl in a circle, singing and dancing without restraint. The only female not participating is an older woman standing outside our circle, glaring at us as if her life depended on it.

"Oh, don't worry about her," the lady beside me says. "That is Elen. She hates anything that might put a smile on her face."

This woman's smile is contagious, and I can't help but grin back at her. She has a mass of red curls flowing around her face, and her green eyes are the color of emeralds. I like her immediately.

"My name is Gerty," she says.

"Anya," I reply.

"Well, Anya. What do you say we give Elen something to talk about."

I quirk my eyebrows and laugh. "What did you have in mind?"

She grasps both my hands and begins twirling us in a circle so fast that the crowd becomes a blur. We fall to a heap on the floor, laughing so hard we can hardly catch our breath.

A group of musicians strikes a tune, and Gerty's mouth falls open with shock when the lead fiddler begins to sing.

He has a beautiful, sonorous voice, and the entire village soon claps along with his words.

"Oh, Gerty, the tease. She leaves a lad hanging.

With no sight nor a word. Of the unanswered question.

She continues to dance and act like nothing is amiss.

But I won't leave here without my due kiss."

A deep blush crawls up her cheeks, and she looks me right in the eye and says, "You'll have to excuse me."

She waltzes right up to the fiddler and plops down into his lap. With a sound kiss on his lips, she says. "Of course, I'll marry you, you silly fool. I just wanted to make you sweat about it for a few days."

The crowd erupts into applause as they kiss again. Everyone except Elen. She pulls her lip up in disgust before sulking into the trees, muttering about sinful acts and damnation.

I turn my attention back to the happy couple, who are now surrounded by well-wishers and receiving slaps on the back as they discuss the upcoming nuptials.

I make my way back to my seat beside the fire just as a little blonde girl tugs on Rowan's pants leg. He leans down so she can whisper in his ear. With an exaggerated sigh, he stands up and begins chasing the girl around the campfire.

More children join in, and eventually, he is overrun with children who jump on his back and pin him to the ground. He begs for mercy as they tickle him, and the small children laugh uncontrollably. The little girl helps him off the ground when the antics are over, and she wraps her arms around his legs in a hug before scampering off after her brother.

A group of men has congregated behind where I am sitting and talking in hushed voices. I strain my ears to hear what they say, and eventually, pick out bits of their conversation.

"The beasts are getting bigger. We saw two of them on the way back to town."

I recognize Lynet's husband, Arthur, as the speaker.

"She has to be stopped before her powers create something capable of becoming a real threat."

"I think we are past that," Simon responds. "I saw one of them attacking a coyote last night. They are already a threat."

A pregnant pause falls over the men and Arthur sighs heavily.

"Inform the families to keep the children close and small animals caged until we can formulate a plan to deal with this threat."

Simon growls before slamming back a cup of wine. "Tonight, we celebrate. No more talk about these creatures until tomorrow."

What in the world was that about? A feeling of impending doom wraps around me. Who is the "She" that the men referred to? Is it

Magda? Has she created something that even now hunts the woods where we sit? I scan the woods surrounding us. The brief feeling of bravery slips away from me like sand through my fingers.

I want to cry. I want to pound my fists against the ground and scream out my frustration about the unfairness of this entire situation. Why can't I just live my life without fear? Why can't I stay with Rowan and these people without constantly looking over my shoulder, afraid of what tomorrow will bring?

Wiping a stray tear from my cheek, I straighten my spine as Rowan walks back to me. He throws an arm around my shoulders and kisses my neck.

The sensation of his lips against my skin sends a thrill through me, and I push down my anguish.

Fuck this. Fuck the fear and the memories and the realization that, at any moment, I might be ripped away from this man and this town. I refuse to let that crippling fear control me any longer. I will live, and I will love, with my whole heart. Not just the scraps leftover after my mother tore it to shreds.

Turning to Rowan, I gaze into his eyes. Only a few inches separate us, and I can see the flickers of the bonfire dancing across the reflection. His amused grin melts away, and he places a hand on my chin.

"Anya. Is something wrong?"

"No. But I have to tell you something. Something I knew from the first moment I saw you but haven't had the courage to say."

His hand falls to my neck and he strokes his thumb against the hollow at the base of my throat. He continues to stare at me but doesn't say anything as I continue.

"I want to stay with you, Rowan. I want to stay in this town and with all these people. I have never felt this alive, and it becomes hard for me to breathe when I think of leaving. I am falling in love with everyone here day after day."

"How about me, Anya? Have you fallen in love with me also?"

"Most of all, you," I say, laying my forehead against his. "You have become as important to me as the air I breathe."

His breath tickles my lips seconds before his mouth crashes against mine. A group of observers lets out loud whoops of encouragement at our public display, but I don't have time to be embarrassed before Rowan grabs my hand and pulls me into the forest, towards his house.

Apparently, walking isn't getting us there fast enough because he begins pulling me along faster until we are nearly sprinting the last few yards to his house. He wrenches the door open and pulls me inside before slamming the door behind us.

After that, a frenzy of grasping hands and clashing lips leaves us both gasping for more.

My dress is the first article of clothing to hit the floor, followed quickly by his pants and shirt. I have nothing under my dress since I have been too embarrassed to ask Lynet for any undergarments.

It doesn't look like Rowan minds my lack of proper garments. His gaze travels down the length of my body, pausing occasionally to study a place he finds particularly appealing.

When he touches me again, sparks of electricity burst under my skin, and I try to keep my knees from shaking. It feels like a lightning bolt shoots through me, traveling from my head to my toes.

"Do you feel that?" I ask, wondering if he is experiencing the same effect. I trail a hand down his chest to his stomach and let myself explore the hard planes of his body. When I begin to lower my hand to his impressive erection, he grabs my hand, stopping me.

"I have wanted you so long. If you start touching me there, I won't be able to do all the things I have imagined since the moment we met."

"What have you imagined?"

"I have imagined touching you here," he says, placing a hand between my thighs and easing one finger between my folds. "And tasting you here." He wraps his mouth around my nipple, and

I practically come out of my skin at the dual sensation of his tongue caressing my tender peaks and his finger inside me.

I grasp his arms and lean into him as he continues to lick and thrust until my body hum's with an invisible need. Pinpricks of light float before my eyes, and I let my head fall back as another finger enters me. The sensation of being filled is all-consuming, and I open my legs further, needing more.

Ignoring his earlier warning, I let my hand wrap around his cock and trail my finger along the tip and underside. He lets out a guttural moan and lifts me so my legs are wrapped around his waist.

"What did I say?" he growls. "You want me to take you so quickly?"

"Yes. I need you. Now." I beg.

I feel empty without his fingers inside me and long to have the pressure of being filled once again. I need him, though. All of him. He lays me on the bed and leans over me.

"Spread your legs for me, Love."

I do as he asks and can't help rubbing myself against him, loving the feeling of his erection between the folds of my sex.

He closes his eyes and takes a few deep breaths. "You are trying to kill me, I think."

"You don't like it?" I ask, suddenly self-conscience.

"The only way I wouldn't like that is if I was dead. But you had better stop before this is over much too quickly. You have no idea how badly I want you, Anya."

His words make me grin, and I push my hips up again. He grasps my hip in a hard grasp and eases the tip of himself inside me.

Holy hell. He is bigger than I realized.

The feel of being stretched consumes me, followed by a burning sensation that makes my earlier arousal diminish faster than a flame being doused in water.

"Wait," I say, putting a hand on his chest. "It's too much. You are too big."

He places his forehead on mine, and we breathe together as the pain recedes and my body begins to relax.

He moves inside me another inch, but the burning returns, and I let out a cry of pain. He takes my hand and brings it to his mouth, sucking on two of my fingers. Then he lowers that hand to where our bodies meet and orders me, "Play with yourself."

"What?" I ask in shock.

"Haven't you ever touched yourself?"

"Well, yes, but only when I was alone."

"Touch yourself now. For me," he says, moving inside of me another fraction of an inch. "It will help."

Blowing out a slow breath, I move my hands to my sensitive nub and begin to rub. At first, I don't understand how it will help diminish the pain, but after a few moments, I am squirming beneath him. The ache of desire turns into a throb, and that turns into a pulsing need.

I push my hips up, and another inch of him is inside me, and then another until he is all the way in and thrusting inside me at an agonizingly slow pace.

He tries to go slow at first, but I don't let him. I match his desperate thrusts with my own while circling my nub, faster and faster.

Rowan buries his head in the crook of my shoulder moments before my orgasm breaks over me.

The explosion of sensation leaves me weak as I climb the crest and fall back down with trembling limbs. The waves of sensation continue to roll over me, and Rowan covers my mouth with his as he drives into me so forcefully, I fear he might break me in two. He groans into my mouth as his orgasm rips through him, and he squeezes one hand on my hip to hold me still as he pumps inside me one last time.

"What have you done to me?" he asks breathlessly.

"To you?" I ask, bemused. "You nearly broke me in two."

All signs of laughter leave his face in an instant. "Did I hurt you?"

"In the best possible way," I reply with a grin.

His grin returns, and he begins to nip at my breast with his teeth. "Well, in that case, I believe I am ready for round two."

I laugh and ease my way off the bed to get dressed. "I have to use the bathroom."

"I'll be here when you get back," he says, propping himself up on an elbow and wiggling his eyebrows.

When I return, he makes good on his promise for another round before we finally lay down to go to bed. As I am dozing off, he tucks a strand of hair beneath my ear and leans forward to whisper into my hair.

"I tried to rescue you, you know."

"What do you mean?" I ask, scrunching my nose. "You did rescue me."

"Not from the mushrooms. I mean before that. At the castle. When I was about sixteen, I thought myself very brave and had this image of myself swooping in and rescuing you from the horrid castle."

I snuggle into him and lay my head on his shoulder. "And why didn't my knight in shining armor do just that?" I ask, loving the feeling of his hand stroking up and down my back.

"I spent years surveying the castle. Watching Magda and waiting. For what? I didn't know. I just knew she had to be stopped and thought I would be the one to do it. But one day, two guards carried a screaming girl down the stairs to the dungeon who was fighting them tooth and nail."

"I remember that day," I say sadly. "It was the end of my childhood."

"As do I. I had never seen anyone with that much spirit."

"That was the day I first met the wolf."

"I couldn't bear to hear you cry inside that cell. After I leaped up and licked your fingertips, I went to the castle to see what could be done about getting you out."

His fingers stroke lazily along my back and circle around to cup my breast. Swatting his hand away, I say, "Tell me what happened."

"I snuck into the castle and located the keys to your cell. They were hanging on a door inside the guard's tower. Unfortunately, Magda caught me just as I was walking out. She has a sixth sense about the locations of the creatures she has made. Me being one of them. She snatched the ring of keys out of my hand and raised a hand to strike me, but the blow never came. I believe she had a small amount of love left in her heart for her children at that time, otherwise I would have been whipped within an inch of my life, or worse."

My eyes must be as wide as saucers at this point. I had no idea this was going on just outside the dungeon that day.

"Then what happened?"

"She told me that if I ever tried to steal from the countess, she would kill everyone I love. And I believed her."

"Oh, Rowan. I'm so sorry."

"It wasn't your fault. If she had threatened only me, I would have tried again. But to threaten the others. She knew I wouldn't risk it. I'm just so sorry. Sorry I couldn't have helped more."

"You helped me every time I saw you. Whenever you sat outside my cell, I felt less alone. Some days, I nearly went mad with loneliness. But you gave me something to cherish."

He leans down and kisses me on the tip of my nose. His arm wraps around my waist and he pulls me snug against him.

"I'll never let you go now that I have you. I have loved you since that first day and every day since."

The feeling of being complete washes over me and fills me with a need to survive.

At all costs.

Chapter 14.

I awake the next day to the feeling of a calloused hand rubbing against my cheek. My eyes remain closed, but I can't help the smile from lifting the corners of my mouth as the hand snakes below the covers. A gasp leaves my lips, and my eyes fly open as the fingers expertly make their way over the tender mound between my thighs.

Rowan is leaning above me with a wicked grin playing on his lips.

"I didn't know how else to wake you. The day is nearly half, and I hate disturbing your rest." His fingers trail back and forth lazily across my folds as he speaks to me. It takes every bit of willpower not to squirm beneath his hands.

"You might try clearing your throat. Or perhaps a nudge on the shoulder to rouse me."

"And miss out on another opportunity to touch you? Never."

"As tempting as that prospect is. I am rather sore after last night's encounter. All four of the encounters, actually."

"Oh, I am sorry, Little Bird." Rowan smiles, not looking the least bit sorry. "Did you need me to kiss it and make it all better?" he says, slipping one finger inside me.

I bite back a moan but no longer can control my hips from rocking forward of their own volition. "You wouldn't dare," I say, appalled and secretly thrilled at the thought of him putting his mouth on me.

Surely, he wouldn't do such a thing.

He dips his head beneath the blanket, and I realize how wrong I am. The feeling of his tongue on me sends me nearly rocketing off the bed.

"Easy now, love. Just relax and spread your legs so I can taste you. I have thought about it more than once, I must admit."

The next lick is just as shocking as the first, but I hold still as he explores the landscape of me.

"You are even more delicious than I could have imagined. Like a sweet pear that has just begun to ripen."

After a few more moments, I grasp his hair with one hand and dig my nails into his shoulder with the other. He throws the blanket onto the floor, and the shock of the cold air nearly steals my breath. He peers up at me with that lopsided grin and places one of my legs over his shoulder.

The sight of him between my thighs is a fucking glorious sight, and a whimper escapes me as he replaces his tongue with his fingers. This man is the definition of sinful but in the best possible way. I don't know how he can anticipate my every desire, but he does it flawlessly. It doesn't take long before I am gasping and pulling at him to join me. I want him inside me when I spill over the edge of oblivion, but he doesn't budge from his place on the bed. He continues his licking and sucking until I am rising to the pinnacle of sensation. My back bows up off the bed, and he reaches up to cup one of my breasts as I spiral off into oblivion.

The moment reality seeps back into my hazy brain, I look down at him, propped up on his hands. My arousal is glistening on his lips, and I am positive no one has ever appeared this self-satisfied.

"I suppose that is another way to wake you up," he says.

"I can't believe you just did that. Do other people know about that? I mean. Has anyone else ever tried that?"

"I suppose one or two other people have given it a go," Rowan replies with a grin.

"Don't you dare laugh at me," I reply, pulling the blanket back onto the bed to cover my cold flesh.

"How in the world would I know that others have done something so... so... so wicked," I finish, unable to come up with another word to describe the sinfully delicious thing he just did to me.

Letting out a bark of laughter, he stands and retrieves my dress for me and tosses it on the bed. "You had better get dressed than before I act on one of the many other sinful thoughts playing out in my brain right now."

"You are insatiable," I tell him and begin getting dressed.

"You have no idea." He wiggles his eyebrows at me, and I can't control my laugh from escaping.

"Do you have something planned for the remainder of the day?"

Peering out the window, I notice the sun is already high in the sky, and we did indeed sleep half the day away.

"We are going hunting." His eyes sparkle, and he begins packing items into a bag. He slings a bow and quiver across his back before sheathing a knife to his belt.

"Hunting? But didn't they get more than enough meat yesterday?"

"We can never have enough meat. What the hunters brought home yesterday is being preserved even as we speak. With all the mouths to feed in the village, any surplus is stored or dehydrated until nothing else can be found. We always hunt when the weather permits, for ourselves and the rest of the town."

I throw my cloak over my dress and add a wool cap which Joy was kind enough to make for me.

"Besides, Little Bird. You need to practice."

"Me? You want me to shoot an animal?"

"Do you have something against it?" His head is cocked to the side while he waits for my answer.

I think about it for several moments before answering. I have never hunted anything before and am not entirely sure how killing an animal will make me feel.

"I would like to try. I can't guarantee there will be a second time, but I'd like to try at least."

Rowan smirks and places a kiss on my forehead. "It's all right if you decide not to pursue this path. Practice will be good for you, though. Just in case you ever need to defend yourself. Learning to use a weapon is useful for more than just hunting."

I think of the mutated creatures in the woods and suppress a shudder. The thought of being able to defend myself against them if needed helps strengthen my resolve, and I grab the belt that Rowan holds out for me. It has several knives attached to the leather, and I tie it around my waist. The weapons attached to my side gives me a small measure of comfort, and I fail to hold back a smile.

Okay. I feel like a badass.

We leave the house with a bag of supplies and head into the forest. On the way to our destination, I get distracted countless times. I often stop to stick my head inside hollowed tree trunks and let my fingers dance over the different textures of the forest. I wait for Rowan to grow impatient with me, but he just leans against a tree and gives me that lopsided grin I have grown to love.

The warmth from the sun's rays melt the heavy icicles hanging from the trees. I reach out and touch a glimmering droplet that clings to a low branch. The single drop quivers on my fingertip before I bring it to my tongue and pop it into my mouth. It tastes of the crisp winter air and fresh bark. I tilt my face to the sky and close my eyes, letting a stray ray of sunshine warm my cheeks. Freedom is better than anything I ever imagined, and I plan to cherish every moment while it lasts. Another drop of water from the overhanging trees falls onto my face, and I smile when the cool liquid travels down my forehead and over my eyelid. If the sun continues this bright onslaught, we will have a muddy walk back to the village.

A good distance from the village, Rowan drops the bag onto the ground and takes the bow from his back.

He sets up a makeshift target out of fallen logs about twenty yards from us and shoots a few practice arrows into the wood. Each arrow hits the desired target and sinks easily into the softwood with a thunk. I watch in fascination as he pulls the bow string taut again, and his back muscles flex under his shirt.

Trying not to look completely incompetent, I study his stance and the angle of his arms. I watch how his fingers grasp the arrow shaft and how far he pulls it back before finally releasing it.

I am practically trembling with excitement as he holds the bow and arrows out to me. "Your turn," he says with a wicked grin.

Licking my lips, I take the bow from him and place an arrow against the string. My fingers fumble for a moment, and he walks behind me to help.

Even through my thick cloak, I can feel his warmth pressed against my back, and I shiver when he leans in to whisper in my ear.

"Like this," he says, placing my hands in the correct orientation on the bow.

His thumb strokes the back of my hand as he goes through the motions of showing me how to hold the weapon. Then he leans in to place a kiss on the side of my neck, and I push back into his hard body. I can feel his arousal through his pants. "You can certainly be distracting when a girl is trying to learn."

"Me, distracting you?" he says, nibbling on my ear lobe. "I don't know what you are talking about. You are the one distracting me."

Letting out a huff of laughter, I focus on the arrow and take a deep breath before aiming and releasing it. The arrow goes wide and sinks into a mound of dirt to the left of the tree, but it comes close enough that I feel a small sense of victory.

He hands me another arrow and guides me through the motions again. When the arrow flies this time, it sinks into the target, and I let out a whoop of satisfaction before running to retrieve both arrows.

I return to him with a grin and a lightness in my heart that is unlike anything I have ever known. This must be what pride feels like. I had never known the emotion before, and it fills me to bursting.

Rowan also has a grin plastered on his face, and he strokes a hand down my hair and plants a tender kiss on my mouth.

"That's my girl."

"Again. I want to do it again."

We practice for hours, and my aim improves with each shot. The last time I pull the string, my arms tremble with the effort and I must concede that the practice session is over.

"Can we come again tomorrow?" I ask, handing the bow back to Rowan as I retrieve the rest of the arrows from the target.

"We can come as often as you like."

"Thank you."

"No need to thank me. I wouldn't dream of being anywhere but here, with you."

Halfway back to the village, Rowan pauses and holds up a hand for me to stop also. Looking at the path ahead, I see what caught his attention.

A grey rabbit is nibbling on a piece of grass only ten yards from where we are standing. Its whiskers twitch as it nibbles, and its glassy eyes survey the surrounding area. It still hasn't seen us.

Carefully, Rowan takes the bow off his back and pulls an arrow from the quiver. Not moving his head to look at me, he slowly hands both to me, being as quiet as possible so he doesn't scare away the rabbit.

My mouth falls open, but I reach out to take them. Does he really mean for me to shoot it? Earlier, I felt confident with my ability to hit a much larger target, but now my confidence deserts me, and my fingers tremble.

Lining the rabbit up with the tip of the bow, I take one deep breath and then another. Finally, I take a deep breath in and hold it.

I can do this.

As I adjust my footing, a twig snaps beneath my boot, and the rabbit swings its gaze in my direction. Our eyes meet for the briefest moment before I let the arrow fly. The only noise in the forest is the arrow slicing through the air and the twang of my bowstring. It doesn't let out a single sound as the arrow pierces through its heart.

Disbelief flows through me, followed by guilt. I have never killed anything before, and my heart suddenly aches for this small, unsuspecting animal.

Rowan lets out a whoop and jumps into the air with an excited fist punch. He grabs me in a fierce embrace before racing forward to retrieve the rabbit.

"Right through the heart, Anya. It didn't suffer at all."

The fact gives me a measure of comfort, and I walk forward to retrieve my bounty. Rowan plucks the arrow out of the animal and holds it out for me. I take it, but my conflicting emotions prevent me from celebrating just yet.

The guilt is warring with the excitement, and I am having trouble sorting the two conflicting emotions out in my head. After a few moments, I land on contentment. I have eaten meat in the past, and even though I didn't shoot it myself, I had no trouble deriving pleasure from the nutrients it gave to my body. This is simply a part of that process. If I hadn't killed this animal, someone else may have, and it would have ended up on their plate instead of mine. It is simply a part of life. At least it didn't suffer. I comfort myself with that thought. I have seen so much suffering in this life. At least, that is one small mercy I could provide to this tiny creature.

Rowan cinches the rabbit into a cloth bag with a rope. He slings it over his shoulder and weaves his arm around my waist as we return to the village.

We walk through town, and Rowan stops several times to chat with people. We pass by the healer's house and Lugh walks outside as we pass by. He beckons us closer and places his warm hands around my frozen ones.

"What is that you have there?" Lugh asks, eyeing the bag with the rabbit.

"Anya shot her first animal. A rabbit," Rowan says proudly.

"Ah, you must allow me to see. I can tell a great deal from the first successful hunt. Come. Come," he says, pulling us inside.

The inside of his house looks like a garden exploded. Even in the middle of winter, plants are perched on the windowsills, and freshly harvested greenery covers every surface. The smell is almost overwhelming, and it takes a few moments before my senses are acclimated to the aromatic environment.

Lugh is a small man. He is even a few inches shorter than me, and I am already on the short end. His black hair is speckled with grey, and the skin of his eyelids is so heavy it's a wonder he can see anything under the overhanging folds of skin. He must be close to ninety, but it is hard to tell with his olive complexion and small stature. He has an easy smile, and the corners of his eyes crinkle up causing his eyes to completely disappear beneath the wrinkles.

He clears a few bowls off the table before bidding us to sit in one of the mismatched chairs. The furnishings can be described as rustic at best. It appears he has little need for finery, preferring to surround himself with the outdoors, even indoors.

Rowan hands the bag with the rabbit out to him, and Lugh pulls the dead critter out of the bag and places it on the table in front of us. Pulling a knife from his belt, he cuts its stomach open with one competent swipe.

I close my eyes to keep the image of the rabbit's insides out of my head. While I may not mind hunting, the preparations afterward are better left to someone else.

After a few moments, I open my eyes and swallow the rising bile that threatens to emerge.

Lugh has the rabbit cut wide open and has its heart held up in front of his face, examining it. He turns it left and right before placing it on a fabric cloth on the table and tying the ends of the towel together. His eyes suddenly look regretful and I wonder what caused such a change in his usually jovial disposition.

He places the wrapped artery into my hands and looks into my eyes with such intensity that I must force myself not to look away. I open my mouth to ask him what he saw, but he holds his hand up to stop me and places a hand on my cheek, still sticky with the rabbit's blood.

"She is coming," he says resolutely.

Those three words are enough to freeze my blood. I drop the package and run.

Chapter 15.

Branches reach out to grab my hair and dress as I run through the trees. A thorn bush slices into the skin of my legs, but I don't care. I keep running. Lugh's words echo inside my head as tears stream down my face. She can't be coming here. I can't go back to that life.

Rowan's voice echoes through the trees as he fights to catch up to me. He is getting closer, and I pump my legs faster to stay ahead of him. When my sides ache, and my breathing is too rapid to sustain this speed, I finally begin to slow.

Rowan catches up to me and tackles me to the ground.

"Let me go," I scream. "I have to get out of here before she finds me."

"No. Anya. You can't run your entire life," he says, pinning my arms above my head.

"Let go of me," I spit out.

"No." His chest is heaving, and his teeth are gritted so tightly I can see his jaw flexing. "You aren't leaving me, Anya."

My breaths begin to slow, and the rapid staccato of my heartbeat returns to normal as I gaze into the innumerable stars above Rowan's head. I can't look into his eyes. I can't bear to allow myself any comfort in this moment. Fear has been my only companion for most of my life, and the familiar feeling slithers back in so quickly that I know it was always there, hiding just under the surface of my elusive happiness.

Rowan cups my face and places his forehead on mine, so I have no choice but to look at him.

"Don't do that, Anya. Don't push me out. You are happy here. We are happy here. Please don't deny yourself that."

His words struggle to break through the walls that have emerged from the depths of my anguish, and a tear escapes the corner of my eyes. It rolls down my cheek and falls to the ground without a sound.

"I have never felt like this about another person," Rowan whispers. "You are like the air I breathe. Without you, I cannot live. I know you feel it, too. Please. Stay with me. We can protect each other."

"You don't know what she's like," I say, wiping another stray tear from my face. "She won't stop until she has me.

"Or until we kill her."

My gaze snaps to his face, and the look is enough to make my heart stop. He is serious.

"You would kill a countess?"

I was going to say you would kill a human, but there is not much about my mother that would constitute as humane anymore.

"If it meant keeping you safe, then yes. I would protect you at all costs. Don't forget that you fell in love with a demonic creature capable of transforming into a weapon at the drop of a hat."

His grin almost makes me smile. He is trying to lighten my mood, but too much is at stake.

"What about the others in town? I can't put them at risk. Not if she is coming for only me."

"Everyone here is at risk while she remains alive. She and Magda are making creatures capable of killing. These creatures are getting bigger and more dangerous with each mutation. It is only a matter of time before it comes to this. At least now we know she is coming, and we will be ready.

He places a kiss on my lips and squeezes my waist. "Please don't leave me, Anya. I couldn't stand it." His eyes sparkle with emotion, and I feel my head nodding against my better judgment.

The thought of staying terrifies me, but leaving him is incomprehensible.

"All right. But I want to continue learning how to hunt. I want to know how to defend myself."

"Deal," he says. His relief is obvious, and I notice his fingers tremble when he grasps my hand.

Pulling me up by one hand, he leads me back into the village, and we go straight to Lynet's and Arthur's house. Arthur will know how to proceed with spreading the word.

After careful consideration, he suggests gathering at sunrise the following morning to address the issue with everyone. He will stand guard for the night along with a few others just in case an attack is closer than anticipated. We agree and walk back home with a sense of impending doom hanging on our shoulders.

Our lovemaking that night is almost feral. There is a sense of urgency that threatens to consume us. It has us gasping for breath as we pull and claw at each other's bodies. With a hard yank, Rowan pulls my hair to expose my neck to his hungry mouth. A growl escapes him as he thrusts into me and devours my throat and breasts with his mouth. I let out a whimper as he slams into me, but I thrust up to meet him with an eagerness of my own. I can feel bruises forming on my hips as he grips my thighs in an embrace that urges me closer with every stroke of his cock.

A scream is caught in my throat, and my body bows back as he strokes my clit and tips me over the edge until I am consumed in a fog of ecstasy and pain that confuses and excites me in equal measure. He bites down on my shoulder and thrusts one more time, so deeply I cry out as he penetrates my core. He pulses, emptying inside of me with one last long stroke.

I wrap my arms around his hips as he rests on top of me. Our breathing is ragged, and the beating of our hearts is erratic, but neither wants to separate our bodies. We fall asleep like this, only to wake up a short while later and ravage each other's bodies a second time.

It feels as if we are both afraid this is the last time and refuse to allow it. This is our time. Our time to enjoy each other and allow ourselves to be in love. Who knows what tomorrow holds? This may very well be the last night we have, and I plan to enjoy it.

When we are both sweating and lying entwined in each other, Rowan strokes my damp hair back from my forehead and says something I would have never expected from him.

"I'm scared. Scared that I will lose you."

"I am sick of being scared. My Mother will not ruin this moment for us, however fleeting it may be."

"It won't be fleeting. We will grow old together and have children together. We will be like Gordon and Fern, playing chess when we have gone wrinkled and grey. I can see it just as clearly as that small freckle on the tip of your nose," he says, touching the tip of my nose with his finger.

A tear trails down my cheek at the image he conjures, and I bravely smile. "I don't have freckles."

"You have freckles on more than just your face," he says, pinching my buttocks.

"I do not," I reply indignantly.

Wrapping his arms around me, he pulls me close, and I love how my body fits perfectly with his. He kisses my hair, and I sigh, loving the moment we are wrapped in. However fleeting it may be...

Chapter 16.

I wake before the sun comes up but lie with my head on Rowan's chest, loving the feel of his even breathing on my cheek. I trace the scar on his shoulder, which still looks angry, but Rowan insists it no longer hurts. Trailing my finger along the wound, I make slow, languid circles, letting my mind wander to what the future holds. Rowan lets out a soft mumble and lets out a yawn.

"Did I wake you?" I ask him.

"You could wake a man from the dead, Little Bird."

I chuckle but continue my perusal of his chest and shoulder. I like touching him. His skin is soft, but his muscles are taut beneath his stomach, and I let my fingers linger there.

He lets out a moan as I navigate the terrain of his body, but my mind is preoccupied, and I can't stop the niggling doubts filtering through my mind.

"How reliable are Lugh's visions?" I ask, hoping that perhaps there is nothing to worry about after all.

"I have never known him to be wrong."

"Just my luck."

I sit up and begin to pull on my clothes, stopping to inspect a sore spot on my waist. A bruise covers one hip bone, and when I point it out to Rowan, his lopsided grin spreads even wider.

"What can I say? You bring out the animal in me. Would you like me to be gentler next time?"

I think about it for a moment but shake my head. "I love the way our bodies are in sync with each other. You give me exactly what I need at the exact moment I need it."

"I feel the same. I have never felt a connection like the one we share."

"What about the other women you have been with?" I ask, genuinely curious and more than a little jealous at the thought of another woman touching him. "Have there been many?"

"Are you truly asking me about my past lovers?" he asks, quirking an eyebrow.

"Well, yes. I am."

He groans and rolls off the bed. Walking to me, he wraps me in a warm embrace, still completely naked. If he hopes to distract me with his body, it's working. But I refuse to let myself be swayed so easily. "Well?"

"You are the only woman I want now, and in the future, but there have been others." His words send a stab of jealousy through me, and I swallow hard to keep the bitter feeling from spilling out.

"I was lonely before I met you. Those women were only temporary distractions from this solitary existence but nothing more. We were destined to be together the moment I met you. You are the starlight to my night sky."

His words melt the fire which burned so hot only moments ago. I don't fault him for taking lovers. I know that many men do. I only hate the thought of someone touching him before me.

"Besides, if I had no experience, I would not have known that you would like this," he said, reaching his hand up my skirt.

My lips threaten to turn up in a smile, but I brush his hand away.

"Well, perhaps you can teach me a few tricks about pleasuring your body so that I might please my next lover," I joke, but the smile instantly falls from his face.

He grabs my face and crushes his lips to mine. "There will be no other," he growls. "You are mine, Anya. Now and forever. Tell me you understand."

"I understand," I gasp as he pushes me up against the wall and bunches my dress around my hips.

He unbuckles his belt and lifts one of my legs and then the other so my legs are wrapped around his waist. With a gasp, he is inside of me, and I grasp his shoulders to keep myself braced against the wall as he begins to move inside me.

His thrusts come faster, and a moan escapes my lips as I climb the now-familiar mountain to ecstasy.

His lips crush against mine before he leans his forehead against mine and stares into my eyes with desire burning hot behind those shuttered lids. "Tell me you are mine," he demands. "And that I will be the only man who touches you here." He leans back and places the pad of his thumb over the sensitive nub, begging for release. When he begins to rub me, my body bows backward seconds before I feel the pulse of release take over.

"You are the only one," I moan out with half-closed lids. My mouth falls open as I begin to climb over the edge. "Faster, Rowan, please. I need you faster."

His movements become frantic, and I can tell he is chasing his release. Our bodies reach that beautiful pinnacle together, and I let out a shuddered breath before collapsing forward into him. He kisses the crown of my head before dropping me back to the ground.

"Only you make me lose control like this."

It is almost an apology, but I can tell by the satisfied look on his face he isn't sorry. And neither am I.

"We should get going. The others will be waiting," I say. "Just let me clean up a bit first."

When we get to the clearing, a large gathering has already arrived, with several more people following behind us. Someone is lighting the bonfire so we don't freeze in the cool winter morning while we wait for the others to arrive.

I rub my hands together and place them deep inside the folds of my cloak to keep them warm. Icy blades of grass crunch under our feet as we walk to the fire, and thick white puffs float into the air with each exhalation of our breath.

The temperature plummeted last night and before long everyone's cheeks are red with the bite of chilled air. Arthur steps to the center of the crowd and clears his throat.

"It has come to our attention that Elizabeth Bathory and Magda may be coming to our village."

Well, okay, no mincing words then. A murmur rolls through the crowd, and Arthur raises his hands to quiet them.

"Lugh has seen it in a vision. We can expect that this is correct. We have also seen the creatures who frequent these woods becoming larger and more of a threat the last few months."

Elen walks forward with her finger outstretched and points directly at Rowan. “I told you to cast that demon out. He is sure to be the downfall of this entire village. Him and his whore," she says, swinging her finger to me.

A feral growl escapes Rowan's throat. Even though her words cut deep, I place a hand on his chest when he tries to step forward.

She continues despite the shocked looks of the other villagers. "They are both the spawn of evil and must be cast out before it is too late."

Arthur's voice rises above the outraged cries of protest.

"There will be no one cast out, and I will hear no more of this talk," he shouts. With one stern finger pointed back at Elen, he says, "You are free to leave at any time, Elen, and none of us will be sadder for it. But you will watch your tongue when making those kinds of accusations where Rowan is concerned. He has been a part of this community far longer than you and is welcome here as long as he desires it."

"But…," she begins.

"No!" Arthur yells. "You may go sit quietly or leave. I will hear no more from you today. We have only forcibly removed two other people from our village, but I have no problem making that a third if you continue with this topic of discussion."

The other villagers nod their heads in agreement, and warmth filters into my heart to see them all forging together to ensure Rowan remains.

Rowan's bunched shoulders relax, and he gives Arthur a nod of appreciation before the conversation continues.

"Now," Arthur says, demanding the attention of the crowd. "We have two options as far as I can tell. We can flee, or we can fight. And I have never been one to back down from a threat."

The crowd murmurs, and more than a few of them nod their heads in agreement.

"This has been a long time coming," Arthur says. "Bathory and Magda have done enough harm to this town already. I won't see us destroyed so she can seek another tool in her bag of black magic. If we back down now, we will be at her mercy now and forever."

The voices of the crowd grow louder, and Arthur yells. "Now, who's with me? Let's bring these two devils to their knees."

Rowan's muscles bunch at the word devils, and I belatedly realize that his mother is also involved. He told me he was used as one of her experiments, but I never learned how he truly feels about her. Does he hate her entirely, or does any part of him still cling to the love he felt before she turned into a tool of destruction? I will need to ask him when we return home.

After the speech, the crowd erupts into applause, and many villagers clap each other on their backs. They throw their fists into the air and gather to formulate a plan. It looks like this altercation with my mother has been a long time coming, and they are itching for a fight with her.

Okay, so we are doing this. All of us.

I pray with everything inside of me that whatever plan they devise will work and not end up with despair.

Gerty comes forward and grasps my hands in her own. Her warm green eyes search my face for a moment before she speaks.

"Are you doing all right?" she asks me with kindness.

I open my mouth to respond, but no words come out. Am I okay? I suppose that is a relative term. Sure, my mother and her sorceress may or may not be on their way here even as we speak. Sure, I spent most of my life locked up in a dungeon, barely hanging onto survival. And yes, my mother did try to murder me and steal my blood to resurrect her long-dead lover. And don't forget the fact that my newfound lover is a fricken werewolf or shifter or half-wolf. Whatever you want to call it. But as I look around the crowd and warmth that flows so freely from them, Elen excluded, I can't help but feel like this is the place I am meant to be.

Rowan throws his head back in laughter and receives a good-natured tussle with Arthur.

"Yes, I believe I am okay," I reply with a smile.

"Just so you know, Elen is the only one who feels the way she spoke earlier. The rest of us truly love having Rowan here."

"I was wondering about that after her damning speech."

"Oh, she is just a bitter old hag with nothing better to do than look down her nose at the rest of us and cast judgment. If you ask me, she should have been thrown out years ago. We would all be the better for it."

I can't help the bubble of laughter that erupts in my mouth. I genuinely like this woman. She says exactly what she thinks without a second thought, and her candidness is refreshing.

"Come now," she says, placing my arm in the crook of her elbow and pulling me along. "I'll introduce you to some of the other women. Rowan has kept you to himself for long enough."

The lightheartedness from moments earlier leaves me, and anxiety takes hold. Sure, I have met some townspeople already, but what if these women don't like me? What if they are like Elen and think of me as only Rowan's whore and spawn of the devil?

Gerty seems to sense my distress and puts a warm hand over mine. "Don't you worry your pretty little head now. These women are lovely. They are sure to love you. You just wait and see."

As we go through the crowd and Gerty introduces me to the others, I realize she is right.

Everyone here is welcoming, and laughter comes easily to them despite the peril that may be imminent. I ask Gerty about this, and she smiles wryly.

"This won't be the first time this town has faced an adversary. We are quite the sight when we all come together to defend what we love. Not to mention Rowan. He is truly a predator when he puts his mind to it. Have you ever seen him in action? The few times I watched him attack, I almost felt bad for the unfortunate beasts who challenged him."

I remember him attacking the four wolves earlier, and Gerty's assessment is spot on. He is a rather menacing adversary when in his wolf form.

Chapter 17.

The pair of socks on the table are a bit misshapen.

Okay. More than a bit, if I am being honest. But that doesn't stop the huge grin from crossing my face as I wrap them in brown paper and tie the package with twine. Lynet gifted me a skein of yarn last week and showed me how to loop and knit it together with needles. Over the last few days, I have wound and then unwound more times than I can remember until something resembling an article of clothing emerged. The craftsmanship needs work, but the second pair was better than the first, and I am confident the next pair will be further improved.

I am giddy with excitement at the thought of bringing Rowan's sisters a gift. They have been so wonderful to me, and I am eager to return the favor. Do they make clothing far superior to mine? Yes. But this is a start, and nothing has ever felt so good.

Rowan tips his head down to plant a kiss on my lips. "Are you sure you don't want me to come with?" he asks with a pout.

I reach up and pat his cheek reassuringly. "I will be fine. You can't be with me every second, can you?"

"Sure I can. Who else will fight off all the eligible young lads in town from swooping in and claiming you for themselves?"

Laughter bubbles over my lips. "You are the only man I want. Er... And possibly Old man Duncan."

Rowan opens his eyes wide in mock horror. "You would really choose Duncan over me?"

“And why not? It takes all my restraint to keep my hands off him as it is. If he were to proposition me, I don't think I could turn him down."

I squeal when Rowan lifts me off the floor and drops me on the bed. His eyes sparkle with mischief as he hovers over me like a feral cat about to pounce on his prey. The growl that leaves his mouth is unexpected, and my eyes fly open in shock.

"Did you just growl at me?" I ask indignantly.

"What can I say? You bring out the animal in me."

Swatting him away with my arm, I climb off the bed and retrieve my parcels. "You aren't distracting me from leaving this house, Rowan. I have gifts to deliver."

He groans and throws his head back on the pillow. "Whatever will I do without you?"

"Likely the same thing you did before I came to live with you."

"It's more fun with you here, though."

"I'll be back in a bit," I say, blowing him a kiss and walking out the door.

I walk to the nearest ladder and swiftly reach the top. The suspended bridge is now my preferred way of traveling across town. The rope under my hands feels comfortable, like I have traveled this way one thousand times before. Nothing compares to how the wind whips through the trees and lifts my hair all around me. It is invigorating and the closest thing to freedom I have ever experienced.

Joy's house is a few trees down from Lynet's, and I knock on her door with three steady raps. She opens the door with a hand pressed to her pregnant stomach and a grin on her face.

"Anya. How wonderful to see you." She looks past me to see if anyone else is behind me. "No Rowan today?"

"No. I just had something to drop off. I hope that's okay."

"Of course. Come in, come in. I just had water on for tea. Would you care for some?"

"Yes, Please. That would be wonderful."

She pours two steaming cups of peppermint tea and hands one to me.

"The girls are down for a nap but this little one has been working himself into a frenzy today. It won't give me a moment's rest to finish my work."

"Oh? What were you working on?"

"Just spinning a few skeins of yarn to bring to the market tomorrow." She points to a spinning wheel in the corner with a half-spun ball of yarn hanging from it.

"That looks fascinating. I would love to learn," I say, taking in the odd-looking contraption.

"I can teach you now if you would like."

"I don't want to impose," I say halfheartedly, but my fingers are already itching to feel that soft wool.

"Nonsense. It's no trouble."

She places me in front of the machine which she informs me is called a spinning wheel. I pick up a handful of wool and bring it to my nose. It smells like a mixture of lavender and lemon with a hint of musk.

"This wool has already been washed several times," she tells me. "We comb all the debris and dirt from it and collect lanolin from it, which is used as a moisturizer."

"How fascinating. I would love to learn that as well."

She gives me a wry smile. "You certainly are eager."

She shows me how to pump the pedal that makes the wheel turn and how to feed the wool a little at a time. The machine spins the wool, creating one tight string of yarn much more durable than the individual thin strands. A smile tugs at my mouth as the yarn begins to wind around a spindle, causing it to grow in diameter.

"Rowan can buy you a spinning wheel when he goes to trade in the city, you know," Joy says.

"Oh, I couldn't ask him to do that. It must cost a fortune."

"It's not terribly expensive. And you would make the money back tenfold when you sell the yarn in the market here."

The idea takes root in my mind, and I rather like the idea of spending my nights behind this rather hypnotic machine.

"Perhaps," I say cautiously, still playing with the idea. "Does he often leave to trade in the city?"

"Every spring." She pauses momentarily and bites her bottom lip as if trying to make up her mind about something.

"He left once, you know, for nearly an entire year when he turned sixteen. He wanted to travel and experience everything this world had to offer. I think he just wanted to leave and clear his head a bit, but either way, he came back ten months later and never said another word about leaving.

I remember that time. I was nearly paralyzed with grief and worry when the wolf didn't visit my cell. Each day, I longed for his company, and each day, I was disappointed. Eventually, I stopped looking for him and resigned myself to the fact that he had died or gone off to another area of the mountains.

"I remember," I whisper.

"Anya. I think the real reason he left was because of you."

"Me?" My eyebrows shoot up, and I stop pumping the pedal to stare at Joy.

"He loved you, even then. When he tried saving you, and his plans went sour, it cut deeper than any of us realized."

I swallow back the tears that threaten to prick at my eyes and look into Joy's watery eyes.

"I'm sorry we didn't try harder," she says. "We should have all tried to save you from that awful place. Can you ever forgive us?"

"Forgive you? You have nothing to feel sorry for. I would have made the same decision if I had been in your shoes. One person's freedom isn't enough to jeopardize an entire town's safety."

"That's what we told ourselves then, but we were wrong. Standing up for what's right is the only way to live. Besides, we have come full circle after all, haven't we?"

"Do you want me to leave? I wouldn't be angry if you did."

"No."

The conviction in her voice is enough to settle my nerves.

"You are one of us now. And Rowan hasn't been this happy in… Well, ever. You are his missing piece, and he would never be whole again if you left."

A tear does spill over now, and I brush it away with my knuckle while taking a steadying breath. I need to change the subject before I make a complete fool of myself and sob all over Joy's wool.

Clearing my throat, I ask, "Did you ever leave? The town, I mean. To see what else is out there?"

"Yes. I left for a few years right after my eighteenth birthday."

"What did you do?"

"I went to school for nursing. I experienced the cultural diversity of a few different cities. I fell in love." She smiles wistfully. "Simon was a solicitor who had just graduated school, and we met at a little café on the outskirts of town. He confided in me he had no desire to practice law or anything of the sort."

She laughs with a far-off look in her eyes. "You should have seen him in a suit. He looked ridiculous. Like someone not at home in their own skin. He was one of the tallest men I had ever met, and the sleeves of his shirts were always just a bit too short."

"So, when did you return?" I ask, enraptured by her story.

"Just after I graduated. Simon and I decided we had enough of the hustle and bustle of the big city. His parents were absolutely furious. But we just wanted to live a quiet life and raise a few children. Plus, this place burrows itself inside your heart, doesn't it?"

I nod, thinking of how happy this town has made me.

"It really does," I reply.

A beam of fading light filters in through the window, and with a start, I realize just how long I have been here.

I stand up and retrieve my gift, which is still waiting on the table.

I hand it to Joy and say, "I wanted to give you something as a thank you for the cloak and the warm welcome."

Joy opens the package and holds the socks up.

My cheeks suddenly burn with embarrassment at the misshapen socks, but Joy throws her arms around me and thanks me profusely.

"The next ones will be better. I have already improved," I insist.

"Nonsense. They are wonderful. Thank you. And tell Rowan hello from Simon and me. We haven't seen him much since you came to town," she winks.

My blush deepens, and I duck out of the doorway.

With the faint glow of sunshine disappearing behind the trees, I decide to wait until tomorrow to bring Lynet her package and make my way down the ladder. Picking up my skirts, I walk swiftly across town. Someone calls out my name, and I turn to see Duncan waving at me from across the dirt path. "Anya, can you spare a moment?"

I look back towards Rowan's house and can see the warmth of a lamp burning in the window. It is tempting to dismiss Duncan and run the remaining distance. It's surprising how much I miss him in my short time away. But I don't want to appear rude, so I hurry over to where Duncan is standing, and he loops an arm through mine. "I need your help with something," he says with a furrowed brow.

"Oh?" I ask, surprised.

"Aye. I just finished this new batch of whiskey and need someone to be my sampler."

I stop and study his face, but he is dead serious, and a chuckle escapes my lips.

"Alright, but just a quick taste. I have to be heading back."

"Of course. Just a quick taste," he says, pulling me towards his house.

I must let my eyes adjust to the dim lighting when we walk through the door. Only one lamp is lit, and the wick is turned down to its lowest setting. He walks over and adjusts the nob so the room becomes blanketed in light. A jug is sitting on the table, and I take a smell of it. One whiff is enough to make my eyes water, and I eye the murky liquid wearily. Perhaps this is a bad idea.

Duncan puts two glasses on the table and pours a generous amount into each. Well, that is more than a small taste.

"Um. That may be a bit much for me."

"Nonsense. Just sit and chat with an old man while you sip on it."

Not sure how to extricate myself from his home without appearing rude, I sit and lift the glass to my lips. Duncan takes the first sip and sighs. "This might be the best yet, Lassie. You should consider yourself honored to taste it before anyone else has a go."

He laughs heartily, and the table rocks forward as his stomach bobs under the surface. I steady the table with one hand and take a sip of the whiskey. It tastes just like his other whiskey, but I make the obligatory "mmm" noise when he asks how it is.

Duncan chats about the whiskey-making process and how he came to live in the Darkest Woods. He goes on for some time, and I politely nod at all the right spots and occasionally ask a question, but my heart isn't in the conversation. I just want to curl up on Rowan's lap and settle in for the night. I take a sip every now and again before the glass comes to my lips empty. I quirk my eyebrows. *How in the world did that happen*?

Duncan fills my glass half full again, and I fall back into a comfortable silence as he prattles on. When he moves to fill my glass a third time, I place a hand on the top and shake my head, which feels a bit foggier than when I arrived. "I really have to be going, Duncan. Thank you for the drink, though, and I will stop again when I have more time." My voice feels thicker than usual, and the S's on my words are a bit slurred. Dear lord, how potent was that stuff?

The old man looks disappointed and even pouts, but a knock on the door has him perking right back up. "That would be Mrs. Brackenhurst. She has come to sample my whiskey as well. Among other things," he whispers.

My eyes widen in shock, and I laugh out loud as he goes to let her in. I excuse myself when she enters and tell her to be wary of the whiskey. It seems rather potent.

The short walk back to Rowan's house is a bit more difficult than it should be, and I slump against the door when I finally arrive. Rowan flings open the door, and I stumble into him, wrapping my arms around his waist to keep myself from toppling over.

"What in the...?" He leans down and takes a whiff of my hair. "Is that whiskey I smell?"

"Old man Duncan wouldn't take no for an answer," I slur.

Rowan's eyes twinkle as he takes in my inebriated state, and he chuckles.

"Saying no to him is a bit of an art. I'll give you some pointers for next time." He leads me to the bed, which I fall into ungracefully and lay my head back on the pillow with a sigh. "This is all I have wanted for the last hour. But that man sure does like to talk when he gets started."

Rowan chuckles and slips my shoes off my feet.

"That he does." He trails a thumb over my cheek. "I missed you."

"I missed you too. Is that silly? That you can miss a person who has only been away for a few hours?"

"Not at all. It means you found the one who holds your heart, and they take it with them every time they leave."

The pad of his thumb glides over my bottom lip, and my tongue darts out to caress the calloused pad before nipping it with my teeth.

Rowan sucks in a deep breath but pulls away. "You should really sleep, Anya. That whiskey packs quite a punch, and you'll have a hell of a hangover in the morning."

I pout. Yes, I know it is childish, but this whiskey has turned my insides to jelly and my core to a burning inferno.

"I just had a thought," I say, propping myself on my elbow.

"What's that?"

"I was wondering if I could try doing that thing with my tongue. You know. The same one you did to me the other night." I flick a finger over the button to his trousers and lick my tongue over my bottom lip. The thought of tasting him causes the heat to spread, and the ache between my legs begins to throb.

"Anya," he growls dangerously. "You aren't in the right state of mind to give yourself to me."

"Well, the way I see it," I say, swinging my legs over the side of the bed and standing. “I have already given myself to you. Multiple times. And whether I was in this state or not, I would want to have you inside me. So, really, you have nothing to worry about." My gaze travels down to where his trousers are beginning to fill out rather nicely with each word I say.

His eyes still look uncertain, but the fire in his eyes tells me he wants this as much as I do. "I'm not sure," he says.

"Well. You tell me when you are sure," I say, nipping his earlobe.

His hands wrap around my waist, and he groans when I reach down to feel him through his pants.

"Anya." His voice is breathless, and I can feel his heartbeat pick up when I trail kisses down his neck.

When I unbuckle his pants, he doesn't resist, but I can tell he is still unsure about this." Don't you want my mouth on you?" I whisper.

"Of course, I do."

"Then let me. I want to taste you."

I let his pants fall and kneel between his legs. At first, I'm not quite sure what to do, so I trail a finger up and down the length of him. He seems to like this, so I wrap my hand around his cock and move it up and down gently. He definitely likes that. His obvious pleasure gives me courage, and I trace a finger over the tip of him. He sucks in a breath when I pull the head into my mouth and swirl my tongue around in circles. A drop of something salty enters my mouth, and I lick it off and let out a moan. His head is thrown back, and his eyes are squeezed closed.

"Fuck. Don't stop, Little Bird."

A thrill of pleasure races through me, and I redouble my efforts to please him. I continue sucking and licking until he is bucking forward and grasping the back of my head in a tight grasp. His hips thrust with each stroke of my mouth until our rhythm becomes a combination of frantic energy. With one last long pump, his hips spasm, and he groans as his salty liquid squirts into my mouth like ribbons of ecstasy.

"Fuck Anya," he says when the last of his seed is in my mouth.

Sitting back on my legs, I swallow and wipe a hand across my mouth. He opens his eyes, and his gaze roves over my swollen mouth. "That was fucking incredible."

"I'm glad you enjoyed it," I say with a grin.

But the truth is, my core is throbbing, and I am tempted to reach down and give myself the same kind of release. But he beats me to it. He flips me over onto the bed so fast, I squeal. My stomach is on the bed, and he bunches my dress up and reaches a hand under it so he can access the part of me that's screaming out for release. He pushes one finger inside me and then another.

Leaning forward, he nips my earlobe and whispers, "My turn."

Chapter 18.

I am helping Lynet knead bread at her house when the first scream comes. It has been nearly two weeks since the meeting about Elizabeth and Magda arriving, and everyone has begun to relax with each passing day.

Rowan is in the forest, patrolling the area with a few other men, and even though he didn't want to leave me, I insisted I would be just fine by myself for a few hours. Lynet looks at me when the guttural scream cuts through the air, and we both reach for the weapons we have kept close the last two weeks. Lynet wrenches the door and steps out first. Her apron is still tied around her waist, and she leaves a dusting of flour on the doorknob.

When I step out behind her, I scan the area focusing on the shocked faces of townspeople but nothing else seems amiss. My gaze sweeps from side to side, surveying the entire town, trying to detect the slightest change, but I come up empty.

Gripping the railing, I wait a heartbeat before another scream reaches our ears. Swiveling my head to the direction the scream came from, my heart drops into my stomach, and my knees begin to tremble.

No matter how many defensive maneuvers I have learned these last few weeks and how impressive my aim may be, nothing could prepare me for the beast that slinks out of the foliage.

The creatures I saw at the castle don't hold a candle to this feral thing. It is like something that crawled straight out of my nightmare and manifested from the depths of hell.

It is ten times larger than the others, with a black skeletal frame and massive winding horns. Even from this distance, I notice the blue glowing orbs set into the bottomless sockets of his eyes. Large, expansive wings stretch out behind him with spikes embedded into every inch of his thorny flesh. I shudder at the sight of the imposing creature, but his menacing appearance is not what captures my attention. No. My gaze is focused on the man clutched in his razor-sharp grasp.

Old man Duncan is swinging his arms and legs to free himself from this unyielding grasp, to no avail. Blood is seeping down his shirt from cuts in his neck where the creature's claws have cut through tender flesh. Duncan still has a bottle of whiskey grasped in one hand and swings it towards the animal's face, smashing the glass bottle to pieces and momentarily blinding him with the fiery liquid.

The creature reaches up to swipe at his face and releases Duncan. The old man ungraciously falls to the earth and rolls a few yards before standing on unsteady legs and sprinting towards town.

He nearly makes it.

The creature whips its forked tail out at an unnatural speed. The barb on the end embeds itself into Duncan's back, causing a scream to erupt from his mouth. The tip of the tail is visible from Duncan's chest, having pierced through his body and emerging from just under his chest bone.

Everything inside me tells me to run to him and help, but the blood leaking out of his mouth tells me that it is already too late.

Within seconds, he drops to his knees, landing face-first into a pile of leaves and dirt. Even at this distance, I can hear the sucking noise as the creature removes its tail from Duncan's back.

Rage boils up inside of me, and the image of his lifeless body spurs me into action. Up until now, it seemed like everything was moving in slow motion. The past few seconds stretched out for an eternity. But now, everything speeds up, and in seconds, I am on the ground with my bow strung taut and my fingers eerily still.

Breathe, just breathe, I tell myself as I release the first arrow.

Others from the town have a similar idea and prepare their weapons to strike. Rowan and the others must have heard the screams because they break through the foliage behind the beast with terror written on their faces. I make eye contact with Rowan across the distance, and the fear on his face momentarily captures my attention. However, when an arrow plants itself into the beast's back, and he lets out a guttural roar, my attention snaps back to him.

Lynet lets loose another arrow from the bridge above me, and the creature whips around to find its attacker.

It almost looks like the creature smiles as his eyes land on me, and he begins stalking towards us. At first, he is on two legs, but then he drops to all fours and moves with slow, deliberate steps.

It appears as if he is enjoying the look of terror on our faces as he gains purchase on our position. The hunters behind him begin to aim their arrows at his back, and in a matter of seconds, his back is littered with them. He lets out a vicious snarl moments before I plant an arrow deep into his eye socket, and he falls to the ground with a heavy thud.

The forest seems to hold its breath in the aftermath of the fight. A strange ringing has started in my ears from the leftover adrenaline. All that is left when the ringing subsides is the eerie quiet of the forest.

Everyone stands perfectly still with wide eyes and trembling limbs, unable to process the enormity of what we have just accomplished. But through the quiet, another sound emerges. The sound of snapping branches. Others seem to hear it also because everyone's attention swivels to the source of the incoming object.

Or should I say objects?

Four more beasts appear through the tree line, larger and more grotesque than the first.

That first animal was just a prelude to the actual threat. These beasts snap their razor-sharp teeth and whip their forked tails around their bodies, eager to begin their conquest.

They all have blue, glowing orbs inside their eye sockets and forked tails, but the similarities end here. Each is their own version of terror incarnate and displays unique traits that separate them from each other. I don't know which is more terrifying between the twisted horns, barbed flesh, and razor claws.

"Well, Magda has really outdone herself," Lynet says above me moments before she crouches and propels herself off the bridge.

In mid-leap, her smooth skin transforms into a white canine body, and she lands on the ground with seemingly little effort. My mouth falls open at the sight of her. I thought Rowan was the only one that could shift into a wolf.

However, now that I think about it. If Magda changed one of her children, why not all of them?

Four other wolves flank me on both sides, including Rowan's familiar black fur. Their bodies are taught and they snap their canines, preparing for the fight.

The fight is inevitable and I force the fear from my mind. Fear will do me no good here. Control is what I need. For years I mastered it and it comes back to me like a finely tuned craft that begs to be released. I count to ten and straighten my spine.

"Well, here goes nothing," I say before charging forward with a dagger in one hand and a bow in the other. The clash of teeth and weapons takes my breath away, and I swing my dagger wildly, just trying to connect with the leathery skin of any beast that is close enough to sink my blade into.

My blade finds its home several times before a claw rakes across my skin, leaving a jagged cut near my rib cage. I look down and place my hand over the wound, thankfully noticing it isn't serious. A few drops of blood leak from the wound, but it could have been worse. Far worse.

The yelp of a wolf draws my attention, and I glance over to see Rowan pinned up to a tree by one of the creatures and razor-sharp claws piercing the skin around his neck. A savage scream echoes through the forest, and it takes a moment to realize it is coming from me.

I run towards him and leap forward to gain purchase as my dagger sinks into the back of the creature. He turns around and whips his claw out, striking me across my face and propelling me back several feet.

The stinging pain across my cheek, however, is nothing to the terror that freezes my veins when I look at Rowan, suspended several inches above the ground, unable to breathe beneath the creature's unyielding grasp.

Adrenaline is pumping through my veins like liquid fire. With that added boost of energy, I jump onto the creature's back and sink my dagger into the creature's neck with a savage cry. I feel like a woman possessed, but I embrace the madness, stabbing and slicing again and again.

Satisfaction flows through me as his blood spurts out from the wounds, and he drops Rowan in his own descent to the floor. I stay on top of him, dripping with sweat and trying to gather my breath. The adrenaline is still pounding through my body, and I turn around to see what destruction lies behind me.

My stomach bottoms out when I see one of the animals, airborne above me. Its claw is outstretched, reaching for me with razor claws. Before it connects, I drop to the floor, hitting my already injured cheek on the frozen ground.

Elen's dead eyes stare back at me from a few inches away. Her throat is ripped open, and the blood has congealed on the cold earth in front of her. Her mouth is stuck open in an agonized expression as if she wants to scream but can't. My mind goes blank as fear threatens to consume me again. So much blood. Elen's dead eyes staring at me. She looks like she is accusing me. This is your fault, her vacant stare seems to say. You should have left when you knew she was coming. A sob breaks free from me but I rest my forehead on the cold earth and force the image from my head. I can't let anyone else die.

Children's muffled cries reach my ears, and I look up to see Lynet's children locked inside their home. They are banging on the windows with tears streaking down their faces. At least they are safely inside for now.

A yelp behind me causes me to turn. Rowan is lifted off the ground by one of the winged creatures and it soars through the air with his fur clutched tightly in its claws. My heart plummets to the floor when the creature releases him midflight, and his body falls through the air for what seems like an eternity.

Running towards him, I make it only halfway before another creature stalks out of the bushes to my left and lunges at me. The blow from his tail is unexpected, and I fly through the air as the pain from the barb slices through my back. When I hit a nearby tree, my vision begins to fade.

I barely have time to feel the second blow before my world goes black.

Chapter 19.

I wake up in a haze of pain and fog.

It takes me a few moments before my vision clears enough to understand why I can't move my arms. They are strapped to a chair with leather bindings so tightly that my hands are beginning to go numb.

Despite the tight bite of leather into my flesh, I pull at the restraints to no avail and curse my predicament.

I am in my mother's dining room, set back a few feet from her table. Candles are lit, and the dishes of food are already arranged as if a great feast is about to start. Porcelain bowls and plates are set on each end of the table. Silverware, which has been polished until it shines, is placed beside a crisp white napkin. The candelabra in the middle of the table has ten red candles burning to illuminate the otherwise dark room. The candles flicker and sway in some invisible breeze, casting shadows to ebb and flow across the stone walls.

Being inside her castle walls again nearly paralyzes me with fear, and I fight harder against the restraints. I try rocking the chair back and forth, but it is bolted to the ground with steel bolts and won't budge.

Trying to swallow down my fear, I think of how to get out of this, and then, an even more terrifying thought comes to me. The sight of Rowan's body falling through the air moments before I blacked out.

Then I remember the sounds. Oh god. The screams of anguish as the creatures wrought destruction upon the village. How many more people perished in that battle? A sob climbs up my throat, and I can't keep back a tear that leaks down my cheek as I try unsuccessfully to keep my fear at bay.

"Well, look who is finally awake."

A voice from the shadows causes me to jerk violently against my restraints. I would know that silky voice anywhere.

"If I didn't know better, daughter, I would think you aren't happy to see me."

Elizabeth saunters into the room with a glass of blood-red wine held in a crystal chalice. She takes a sip and closes her eyes to savor it.

Her pale skin seems even more ghastly under the faint candlelight and stands in stark contrast against her crimson gown. Her dark hair is coiled into a severe bun at the base of her neck, and an impressive necklace of rubies and diamonds is affixed tightly around her throat. The gems shimmer as she walks towards me, and I try to look anywhere except at her impassive face.

"And after all the work it took to find and bring you back to me. I almost think you are not appreciative of all my efforts."

She saunters right in front of me, trailing a finger across my cheek as she goes by. She circles around the table and sits directly across from me. Her imperious posture leaves no doubt she is royalty, and she uses every inch of that stature trying to intimidate me.

Unfortunately, it is working.

A few seconds go by with us simply staring at each other. Her lips turn up at the corners before she rings the silver bell on the table, indicating she is ready to be served.

Two servants walk in with covered platters, which they place on either side of the table. In a synchronized movement, they lift the lids off the platters, and I brace myself, expecting something truly horrid to be placed underneath. When all that sits on the dish in front of me is a bowl of soup, I let out a sigh of relief.

My relief is short-lived. I squint my eyes at my mother when she takes a spoonful of her soup. Something about her actions is off. She is too confident and seems to be gloating about something, but I can't tell what.

"Dig in. The soup is delicious."

She draws out the S on the last word and sounds like a snake about to strike its prey. A bubble of laughter escapes from her, and she holds her napkin to her lips to hide her smile.

"Well," she asks, "Aren't you going to eat?"

"I'm not hungry," I grit out through clenched teeth.

She ignores my remark and rings the bell again. A servant comes forward to help me eat, but when they lift the spoon to my lips, I turn my head and clench my lips shut.

My mothers' eyes grow wide, and she cocks her head innocently.

"What's the matter? Don't you like the taste of wolf?"

The smile she has tried keeping away breaks from her lips, and maniacal laughter erupts from her mouth. She throws her head back and pounds on the table. Tears stream down her face as she cackles like a mad woman.

I look down into the creamy stew, which has bits of meat floating around in it. Every ounce of blood drains from my face, and an electric current shoots through me like lightning.

My scream is so loud it shakes the crystals on the chandelier. Tipping the chair from side to side, I try to unbalance it so it might topple over and break the wooden arm I'm strapped to.

If I can get my hands around her throat, she is a dead woman.

My foot kicks out and connects with the bowl of soup, sending it spiraling into the air. The contents end up splattered across the entire table, with a generous amount ending in my mother's lap.

She wipes a streak of broth from her cheek, and if looks could kill, I would be six feet under. With the regality of a queen, she saunters over to me. My breathing has become ragged from my tantrum, and my wrists burn from where the straps are digging into my skin. Her breath tickles my ear when she bends down to whisper in my ear, and it takes every ounce of energy I have not to turn and rip her cheek open with my teeth. Instead, I grit my teeth so tightly they might break.

"He was still alive when we began to cut the meat from his bones. He had a long and excruciating death."

Every word out of her mouth feels like a knife driving into my heart.

Rowan is dead. And it is all my fault. I should have left when Lugh said she was coming to the village. And now people are dead because of me. Every bit of the fight goes out of me, and I slump forward in the chair, letting tears streak silently down my face.

"Clean her up and bring her to my bedchamber," she tells the servants. "We have unfinished business to settle."

I don't even fight as the servants unstrap me. I sit dazed in my chair as her words play over in my head again and again.

Rowan is dead.

The thought is too big for me to consider, so I do the only thing available to me.

My mind goes numb.

Every single thought floats out of my brain, and I hang limp as four servants drag me off to my mother's bed chambers. I can't live without him. He has only been in my life for such a short time, but the thought of surviving without him completely paralyzes me. He is the one who taught me how to live. After an entire existence of barely surviving, he taught me what it feels like to be whole, and I can't imagine that without him beside me.

His words the night I tried to flee come back to me. I want to grow old with you. Tears begin streaming down my face as the thought of a world without him begins to take shape in my mind. Why, out of all the people in the world, did he have to be taken from me?

I know why, of course. Because of my mother. She took this slim moment of happiness from me for her own sick purposes. She went stark raving mad when her lover was killed but thought nothing of taking the only person I cared for. How selfish can she be? How horrible of a person to remove someone who means everything to me.

The closer we get to my mother's room, the more my hatred grows. My chest begins to heave as I allow myself to absorb this hatred into my very soul. It burns hot like a thousand tiny flames, licking at the core of my existence until my cheeks flame hot, and it feels as if fire is beginning to erupt from my core.

She did this. She took Rowan from me, and I will not go down without a fight.

The door is opened by a female servant, who steps aside to let us enter. When we enter the room, I look first to the left and then to the right. Mother is on one side of the room, standing next to the hearth and drinking her damnable wine with a smirk. Magda is on the other side of the room, mixing a concoction inside a mortar and pestle, uttering an incantation under her breath.

Since the restraints are no longer around my wrists, I use the few seconds of freedom to wipe the smug look off my mother's face.

I throw myself at her.

The servants are so startled they don't have time to grasp me again before I am on top of her. The shock on her face makes whatever punishment this will produce completely worth it. The wine glass slips from her hand and shatters on the floor as my hands circle her neck.

I feel like an animal possessed, but I don't care. I scratch and claw until her face is bleeding, and it takes all four servants to pull me off her.

Adrenaline is coursing through my veins, and my chest heaves with the exertion as the lingering energy still flows through me.

With more than a little satisfaction, I notice her hair has come undone, and I am grasping a scrap of her dress that I managed to tear away while the servants were pulling me back. Her cheeks are bright red with anger, and a trickle of blood is flowing freely down one of her cheeks. She uses the tip of her finger to wipe away a drop and holds it up to inspect before fixing that glacial gaze on me.

"Tie her to the bed."

Even though she has just been assaulted and is trying to reign in her fury, her voice does not quaver in the slightest. It is infuriating, and I pull against the hands holding me to see if I can strike her smug face once more before they detain me. No such luck, unfortunately.

I am thrown onto the bed, and even though I thrash and buck, it doesn't take them long to restrain my limbs to the posts. Spread out like this, I suddenly feel vulnerable and more than a little scared.

Images of my mother's past victims come back to me with startling clarity, and I swallow down the scream that is threatening to break out of my chest. My muscles quiver as the fear subsides and is replaced with a tiredness I haven't known since my time in the dungeon. The short-lived victory of assaulting her suddenly feels like a terrible idea as she walks forward and hovers over me.

The fury is pouring out of her eyes like a liquid fire and her lip curls up in disgust as she looks down at me.

"I will tell you what happens now, dear daughter. You will willingly comply with our plan, or else I will murder each one of those villagers while you watch. I can imagine you got to know many of the people there. You wouldn't want their blood on your hands now, would you?"

Her words freeze my trembling heart, and a cold sweat breaks out across my skin. Does she truly mean it? Would she be so evil as to murder more innocent people? But I know the answer. Of course, she would. I have seen her commit heinous acts much worse than that. I'm sure she can do it, especially with those mutated beasts at her disposal.

"Do you need some persuasion? I can have one of them fetched now so you can watch them die in front of you if that is what it takes."

I shake my head. The thought of watching another person die suddenly makes me feel very tired. Enough people have perished because of my need for freedom. The images of Duncan and

Elen's lifeless eyes have burned into my mind, and hot tears leak down my cheek. No one else will die because of me. Even as the tears begin to flow freely, I steel my voice.

"Do what you brought me here for."

I have to turn away as my words send a look of triumph over her face. Fighting against this won't do any good, and I conjure up an image of Rowan to remove my mind from things to come. I think of his amber eyes and that lopsided grin, letting the image transport me far away from here.

Magda walks over to the bed and places a bowl on the side table before sitting beside me. She skims a hand down my face, leaving traces of whatever substance she has prepared for this ritual. Ancient words flow out of her mouth and her hazy eyes roam over my body as she recites the incantation. Her finger pauses mid-stroke, and her words stop as she cocks her head to look at me.

Leaning in, she sniffs my hair and moves lower to place her ear on my stomach. Letting out a grunt, she stands up and turns away from me.

"This ritual cannot proceed," she tells my mother.

"Whyever not?" Elizabeth replies indignantly. 'We finally have her here, and she is willing. Just as you said."

"You are correct," Magda replies. "But she is no longer innocent. You need the blood of an innocent. She has lain with a man since she was last here."

My mother's icy gaze swivels to me, and she clenches her fists together so tightly that blood begins to drip from where her fingernails are piercing her skin.

Oh shit. This won't be good.

"You filthy whore."

Her voice is low at first and then becomes a shrill cry of anger as she advances towards me. "You have ruined everything so you could rut like an animal with the first man who showed interest in you."

Her hand comes up to strike me, and I have no way to defend myself as her hand connects with my cheek.

My cheek burns with pain, and the coppery taste of blood invades my mouth from where my teeth have cut my cheek. She raises her hand again to deliver another blow, but Magda's words stop her arm in midair.

"There is another way."

Mother whirls around, fixing her maniacal gaze on Magda. "Tell me."

"Not only has your daughter lain with a man, but she is also with child."

Chapter 20.

A strange buzzing begins in my ears, and each breath becomes harder than the last. With child? That can't be right. Can it? I think back to the past few weeks and realize I could indeed be with child. The thought hadn't occurred then, but now it seems foolish that I never considered it.

Rowan's beautiful amber eyes cross my mind and I have to squeeze my eyes shut to keep back the flood of tears. His words of love and our future comes back to me in full force. He wanted this. I know it. Now he isn't here, and everything is ruined. I have never felt as alone as I do now, even chained up in her dungeon. That seems preferable to the misery being inflicted on me now.

"You are sure?" Mother says, glancing at me as if she could see the evidence herself.

"Oh, yes. I can hear its heartbeat fluttering against her womb."

"Well then. I suppose we have a use for you, after all. At least until the babe is born. A baby is the purest form of innocence, and their blood will do just as well as yours."

She sits in her chair and picks up a new glass of wine that has been set out for her. Her expression looks almost bored as she runs a finger over the cut on her cheek.

Flicking a hand to a guard, she instructs him, "Take her outside into the courtyard and dole out her punishment for the entire castle staff to see. Keep the wounds to her back so you don't accidentally kill my future grandchild. As much as I'd like to wield that whip myself, I have other matters to attend to."

Then comes that damnable laugh again.

My hand lands on my stomach when I am untied. The thought of a child living within feels unreal and makes me a little dizzy. Will it have Rowan's brown hair and amber eyes? I force the thought away. It's no use wondering about such things since it will hardly matter anyway. This child will be a tool used by Mother and Magda. Just like me.

The guard shoves me roughly along through the corridors and into the courtyard. It has begun to snow again and thick tufts of snowflakes fall all around me and stick to my cheeks. A thin layer has blanketed the outside world since I was outside last. It seems like a new world. It feels like a new world also. Colder and full of despair. The biting wind whips my hair around my face as I am tied up again, this time to a pole. I don't have it in me to fight. It will only make this worse. The ropes are pulled so taut that my shoulder strains to keep from popping out of the sockets.

Servants have been summoned to watch the punishment, and they stand huddled under a copse of trees a few yards away. Some look terrified for me, others look intrigued. A few of them look indifferent, as if they see this every day. Maybe they do. Perhaps they have witnessed atrocities so often that the sight of a girl being beaten no longer fazes them.

A guard walks forward with a whip in his hand and a devilish smile on his face. "Oh, how the mighty cherished daughter has fallen from grace."

I remember his face from the dark halls of the castle. He has always made my skin crawl. On more than one occasion he has forced the female servants to do unspeakable things against their will while others watch.

Holding my head as high as I can manage, I spit in his face. It is the only act of defiance available to me and the surprise on his face makes it worth it. The shocked look on his face is short-lived, however. His grin gets even wider, and he wipes off my spit with the back of his hand and licks it off. "I'll have a better use for that mouth after I have finished whipping you within an inch of your life."

He waggles his eyebrows and grabs the crotch of his trousers as he adjusts his obvious arousal. The thought of this man touching me is enough to keep any further insults from leaving my mouth. The guard walks behind me, and the sound of the whip hitting the ground has me trembling before it even touches me. I have seen what comes next.

Even though I am determined to keep from crying out, the first lash across my back rips a scream out of me despite my attempts to stay quiet. It tears through my flesh with an intensity so profound I nearly soil myself. My legs tremble with the effort it takes to remain upright and the ropes pull at my arms.

It feels like flames are dancing across my back, and blood begins to trickle down my back. He flicks the whip against the ground, and the thought of another lashing nearly makes me pass out. I know his purpose is to inflict fear as well as pain, and I try to be brave. I want to curse him. I want to spit in his face again and hold my head up high. But every ounce of courage flees me, and the tears begin to fall.

I have been whipped a few times in the past, but nothing comes close to the pain this man inflicted on me. When I look back, I can see why.

He has attached a spiked ball to the end of the whip, which now drips with the blood he has just drawn from my back. Oh, dear god. He is going to kill me with that torturous instrument. Even though I try to pull my eyes away, my gaze refuses to focus on anything other than the man raising the handle into the air as he prepares to dole another blow.

I squeeze my eyes shut, anticipating the next agonizing blow. A gurgling scream of pain has my eyes flying open again.

The guard, who was so arrogant a moment ago, is now lying on the ground with an arrow through his neck. He is grasping at the shaft, trying to dislodge it from his throat. Blood seeps out of the fatal wound as he gasps for breath like a fish. In a few moments his eyes roll back into his head and his thrashings stop. The servants run away when they see the dead guard, afraid they may be next. Or even worse, accused of being the one to deliver the fatal blow.

My eyes fly to the direction the arrow came from. I nearly faint in relief when Rowan walks out of the woodlands and sprints towards me. He has a bandage around his ribcage and is favoring his left leg, but that doesn't stop him from reaching me in mere seconds.

One side of his face is covered in a large bruise, but he has never looked more beautiful. He takes a knife out of his belt, and in two swift cuts, my arms are free, and I am holding onto him like my life depends on it.

We are both trembling and when Rowan draws me into a hug, I let out a cry of pain as his arms squeeze the wound on my back. His eyes darken when he inspects the lashing, and a snarl begins low in his throat.

"We need to leave," he insists, pulling me towards the woods.

"No," I say, removing my hand out of his grasp. "She needs to be stopped. Or we won't ever be free. We can't wait for those creatures to return and wreak havoc again."

I keep the knowledge of the baby growing inside of me to myself for now. If he knows about it, there is no way he will let me stay and make a stand against my mother.

His expression is torn, and he keeps glancing back and forth between the castle and the woods. He finally groans and grits his teeth so hard his jaw flexes. "Fine, but you stay out here while I go inside."

"No. We do this together."

"You are in no condition to fight."

"Neither are you." I spit back.

"Well, lucky for us both, I brought backup."

At that moment, the snapping of branches echoes through the area and five men walk towards us. It is Arthur and Simon, followed by three other men from the town. All are armed with bows, arrows, and knives. They walk towards us, breathing heavily. "You could have waited for us," Arthur says to Rowan.

"There wasn't time. If I had waited, Anya's back would be a bloody mess by now."

Arthur just grunts in agreement and eyes the castle with dread. "Well, what's your plan now that we are here? Are we just going to barge in and demand she surrenders?"

"We have to cut off the source of her power. Without that, she is not a threat," I say assuredly.

"Magda?" Arthur asks with raised eyebrows.

"Yes, Magda," Rowan replies

"And how do you suppose we will do that?" Arthur says with raised eyebrows.

"We have to kill her. It's the only way she can be stopped. A prison won't hold her. Not with her limitless powers."

"But she is your mother," Arthur says.

"She stopped being my mother the day she used her children as test subjects. Now she is just another threat who almost ruined everything."

I have no love for the woman, but the thought of him killing his mother sits heavy in my chest.

He places a hand on my cheek reassuringly.

"How many innocent women have they killed? How many more will die if we stand by and do nothing?"

I know he is right, and agree with a nod of my head.

"I know how to get to her," I tell them.

I have spent my entire life living in the shadows here and know every passageway.

"This way," I say, leading them around the castle's base, where a door is partially hidden by leaves and snow. Brushing away the debris, I swing open the heavy door and it falls open with a thud. It is dark inside, but I know this passageway so well I could travel it in my sleep.

It is evident by the stale air and scampering of rats' feet that this passage is not frequented often. The sound of heavy footsteps follows me as I make my way through the stone corridor. I trail my hands along the wall to keep myself oriented in the right direction. The wound on my back pulses with pain, but I continue on, knowing this nightmare won't end until these women have been stopped.

Rowan's hand grasps mine in the pitch-black, squeezing twice for comfort. I reach up and, finding the tender skin of his arm. I pinch him as hard as I can.

"Ow," he yells. "What in the world was that for?"

"Why didn't you tell me your sisters could shift also?" I whisper-yell back.

"I'm sorry, but it wasn't my secret to tell. No one else in town knew until that moment."

A bit of indignation goes out of me, but I press on anyway, needing the conversation flowing to keep my mind off what awaits us.

"How did they learn that you could and not them?"

He groans out loud, and Arthur laughs.

"Now that's a great story," Arthur says.

"Well, now I need to know."

Rowan sighs in resignation. "I was trying to impress a girl."

My laughter echoes through the corridor, and I hold a hand to my mouth to cover another burst that threatens to erupt.

"You didn't."

"It did not have the desired effect. As you can imagine."

"I imagine it didn't," I say with another snort of laughter.

"I was only thirteen. It seemed like a good idea at the time. Lynet gave me a smack upside the head afterward when she had to explain to the entire village her brother was a wolf shifter."

The other men in the tunnel chuckle, and I bite back another laugh as we begin to near the end of the tunnel.

A flicker of light in the distance outlines the threshold of a closed door. When we finally reach our destination I straighten my back and turn the handle. The hinges groan as I push the heavy door open. I hold my breath to see if anyone heard the noise, but no one comes to investigate, so I wave the men forward. The room is empty and dark when we enter. The empty bathtub sits in the center of the room and the mirrorless vanity is against the back wall. My stomach sinks when I remember all the times I have been brought to this room to be trussed up like a doll.

Rowan walks to the other side of the room where a green cloak is hanging on a peg. He lifts it off the hook and brings it to me, wrapping it around my shoulders. His lips graze my cheek and he looks right into my eyes.

“You never have to come back here after today,” he whispers in my ear.

His words give me a measure of reassurance and I lean into him for strength.

"How will we know where to find her?" Arthur asks.

A scream cuts through the air, and all the men look at me with wide, shocked eyes. That sound has become so familiar to me that I just shake my head and sigh.

"They will be in Mother's bedroom."

Chapter 21.

Another scream emerges just as we reach her room. The door is not locked, and swings open without a sound.

The sight before us is ghastly. Mother is using one of her favorite torture devices on a trembling girl strapped to a high back chair. She has on an iron glove that fits snuggly over her hand. On the tips of each finger are razor-sharp spikes, which she is currently dragging down this girl's arm. Drops of blood are oozing down her arms as the spikes rip into her tender flesh.

The girl is trying to scream again but a gag has been placed over her mouth and snot runs from her nose. Magda places a bowl beneath her arm to collect the droplets as they fall. When she turns around to retrieve something on the side table, she notices us in the doorframe.

"It appears we have company, Elizabeth."

Magda's appearance is shocking. It looks as if she might die at any moment. If she seemed old before, now she seems one step out of the grave. Her skin is so thin it is nearly transparent. Bloodshot eyes peer out from under drooping eyelids, and her sunken cheeks show sharp cheekbones.

The extent of her dark magic is undoubtedly taking its toll on her. She can barely manage to remain upright, even now. A wet rattling noise crackles through her chest with every breath, and her lips have turned a deep purple hue from lack of oxygen.

Elizabeth turns to us with half-crazed eyes and her gloved hand is dripping with blood. When she sees us, her mouth drops open in shock, and her skin loses some of its color. She moves over away from the trembling girl, and with horror, I realize it is Olivia. Her terror-stricken eyes are wild and seem to be begging me to help her.

The room remains silent for a few agonizing heartbeats before Rowan steps forward. "Was it worth it, Magda? Giving up everything in this insane pursuit of power."

"I regret nothing," the old woman croaks. "I would gain unlimited power if it were not for the constraint of this wretched mortality. I still have time to remedy that, with the help of your precious lover."

"Your time has run out, Magda. We won't allow you to hurt another innocent person."

"I would like to see you try to stop me."

She reaches up and balls her hand into a fist. When she opens her hand a glowing orb rests on her palm and she leans in to whisper to it. Her words are too faint for me to hear but whatever she says causes the temperature in the room to plummet. My teeth begin to chatter as an icy swirl envelops us and my breath comes out in frigid puffs of white air. Whatever invisible connection she wields is enough to cut off Rowan's air supply, and he grabs at his throat, trying to suck in the air he so desperately needs.

Arthur and his men advance to detain her and hopefully break the connection, but she throws up her other hand, and all the men fall to their knees in pain. Magda throws her back and begins chanting to maintain the power, but the effort to hold the spell causes her arms to tremble. Her skeletal frame seems to wither even more as the seconds go on, and the skin on her face begins to shrink back, revealing the ivory bones and muscle underneath. The sight is grotesque. Her body is literally consuming itself as she calls on the last of her energy to destroy her own son.

I watch in shock as her entire body begins to hum with spent energy, and the bones in her legs snap, unable to hold her frame up any longer. She twists and groans in pain while the transformation takes place, but still, her chanting continues.

While she is distracted by detaining the men, I throw myself at her, trying to break the deadly connection. Rowan's face is turning crimson as he becomes desperate for air and the other men are lying on the ground covering their ears. I need to do something before they die. The glowing orb in her hands burns brighter and I fling myself at her, trying to knock it out of her hands.

When my hands contact her arms, I know immediately that something is wrong.

Her flesh feels like rotting fruit. My hands sink beneath the surface before I have a chance to pull back from her. A black ooze coats my hands from her rotting skin. I draw back in shock and try to wipe the black substance from my hands but only manage to smear it across my skin. It is sticky like tar and clings to me no matter how furiously I try to remove it.

While I am trying to process the depths of this depravity, the black ooze begins to seep out of the holes in her skin where my hands had been moments earlier. I back away quickly, trying to distance myself as much as possible.

Then comes the smell.

The odor comes off her in waves and is so strong it makes my eyes water. It smells like rotting corpses and excrement. I'm certain that I will never encounter something this vile again. I try to wipe it from my hands again so I can cover my nose, but it remains stubbornly stuck to me. It takes every ounce of my willpower not to vomit.

Three winged silhouettes penetrate the wood floor and swoop down to her, landing near her crumbling body. They are transparent but their shape indicates they are the shape of a horse with sprawling wingspans that brush the ceiling. One reaches out and pulls a black shadow from inside her chest, and she lets out a shriek of protest.

"You can't," she cries. "I'm not finished yet. I only need a little more time to complete my task."

"Your time is done, old woman," the darkness whispers.

Apparently she made a deal with these creatures and payment has finally come due.

With one last tug, it rips a shadow out of her chest, and her body lands on the floor with a thud. Her remains look more like a rotting corpse than a woman who was alive only moments ago.

Her shadow struggles as they carry her away. Moans fill the room as she tries to break free but the phantoms hold her fast as they move across the room. The black ooze on my hands follows the procession, melting into her shadowy figure as they absorb back into the floor from where they came. I hold my hands up but no hint of the foul liquid is left behind.

All five men are on the floor, panting with shocked eyes and wide-open mouths.

My mother is looking at the spot where Magda's body lies, and she reaches out as if she wants to touch it. She begins edging towards the door, but I stop her dead in her tracks when I swing my gaze to hers.

Her self-assured gaze is gone, replaced by a look of uncertainty, and she keeps glancing between me and Rowan. I take a dagger off the table and walk to her slowly, enjoying her flinch when I stare down my nose at her as she has done to me so many times. The dagger seems to burn hot in my hand as I clench it. The need to watch her suffer nearly chokes me, and my muscles tremble with the effort it takes not to plunge the blade into her stomach.

"You made me think he was dead."

"It's easier to make someone compliant when they think they have nothing left to lose."

I slap her across the face so hard her head jerks sideways. Her cheek is scarlet when she turns back to face me, and I notice with satisfaction that she looks afraid. I'm sure she isn't used to people striking her, and I am tempted to do it again. Instead, I lean in close and whisper in her ear.

"You will know what it has been like to be trapped in a prison, just the same as you have done to me. The endless days will drive you mad, and you will receive no comfort other than the bare necessities to keep you alive until you die, a slow, lonely death."

With each word, she seems to shrink back until her shoulders are hunched and her once proud stature is turned in on itself. Arthur walks forward with a length of rope and binds her hands.

“Take her to the prison,” I say.

He gives her a shove forward and leads her to the doorway.

"Wait," I call out.

I pick up a small handheld mirror and hand it to Arthur. "Make sure this is the only thing in the cell with her."

He grunts his acknowledgement and pushes her forward into the corridor.

"Last cell on the left," I call after them.

The thought of her in the same cell she kept me in for years brings tears to my eyes, and I fall to my knees and begin to sob. Never in a million years did I think my mother would one day take my place. It is more than she deserves, but I don't have it in me to kill her. No matter how horrible she has been to me.

She can spend the rest of her life locked away in that pitiful cell, knowing that I am free.

I hope she thinks about me often.

Maybe she will even feel sorrow for treating me like an animal. Somehow, I doubt that, but I know one thing for certain. I will not let her invade my thoughts again.

She will have no place in my future. She is my past, and I will leave her where she belongs.

Rowan sits next to me and places an arm around my shoulders while my sobs quiet. I stand from the floor and pick up the ring of keys, which my mother always keeps on a peg near the doorway. One key is larger than the rest, and I remove it from the ring and place the others back.

Olivia has taken in this entire thing with shocked eyes but remains quiet while everything has transpired. I walk to her, and Rowan cuts the ropes that bind her hands and legs.

Her trembling hands come to her mouth, and a silent tear falls down her cheek. The scratches on her arms have already stopped bleeding. They were only shallow cuts. Thankfully Mother had just begun her torture and wasn't able to inflict to much damage. I hand her the key to the cell where my mother will be held and clasp her hands in mine. She looks down at our combined hands and gazes back up with a question in her eyes.

"You are responsible for her now. Make sure she never leaves that cell and gets only what she needs to survive. Can you do that?"

She nods, and some of the fear I saw earlier vanishes from her face. "I... I won't let her hurt anyone else. I promise," Olivia tells me with a trembling voice.

I believe her.

Chapter 22.

We bury Elen and Duncan as soon as the ground thaws. Their graves have been placed on a grassy hill just outside of the village. A thick fog blankets the area, wrapping us in a cocoon of serenity, befitting the occasion.

Lugh says a few words, and we all bring an offering to thank them for their sacrifice that day. Tears roll down my cheeks when I think of Duncan's rosy cheeks and booming laughter. He shouldn't have died for this. The entire village has taken his death hard but we are finally picking up the pieces and returning to normal life.

Rowan and I are the last to stand before the graves, and I kneel down to place a grey feather on each of the mounds of earth. Feathers represent protection, and I picked these gifts to help them on their journey to the afterlife, if that is where they end up. I still have not decided exactly what I believe happens when we die, but that is the beauty of indecision. It leaves endless possibilities open to us. One day, I may have a more definitive grasp on my beliefs, but for now, my mind remains open to the unknown. I have witnessed enough in my life already to know that anything is possible and not to discount anything.

We walk back home in silence, both lost in our feelings of melancholy. The weather has warmed enough for buds to begin blooming on some of the trees. The edges of the dirt path are damp from the previous night's rain and the smell of moist dirt is heavy in the air. We walk past Duncan's house and I can't help the sadness that envelops me at his departure. He will be missed.

When we are inside, I place my forehead against the closed door with a sigh.

Rowan walks up behind me and wraps his arms around my stomach. He smooths both hands over my protruding belly and kisses the side of my neck. A shiver of desire courses down my spine, and goosebumps break across my skin. Even after months together, I have still not gotten enough of this man touching me. Maybe I never will. He rubs circles over my belly and sighs into my ear.

"They feel feisty today," he says, nuzzling my neck again.

"I couldn't sleep all night. I believe they want out already, and there are still four months left to go."

It's hard to believe that much of my pregnancy remains. My stomach already looks like I swallowed a melon. I can't imagine how big it will be towards the end. That is the consequence of carrying twins.

I had begun to have suspicions due to my advanced growth, but last week, Lugh held a hand to my stomach and whispered in my ear, "They are healthy," confirming my suspicions.

"Have you thought of names yet?" Rowan asks me.

"Not yet, "I sigh. The idea of something so profound gives me anxiety. What if our children hate whatever we pick for them? It is something that will remain with them their entire lives. I just want to make sure they like whatever we choose.

Rowan seems to sense my anxiety and whispers in my ear. "Perhaps we should wait until they are born and see which names fit them."

I look at him and smile. "I like that idea."

"If they come out with tails and fur, we should give them something more fitting to a canine."

Terror seizes my heart, and I look up to see if he is joking. A wide grin is on his face and I smack his stomach.

"That's not funny. What if they really do have some of your... Erm… Special abilities?"

"My sisters have had a brood of children, and they have all come out right as rain," he says, kissing my head.

I relax into him and resist the urge to give him one more smack for scaring me.

My life here has been incredible these last few months, but some decisions, even small ones, cause me to waver.

The world is made up of so many decisions that occasionally, I feel the need to consider all the possibilities.

It is from my time in the dungeon. I had barely any decisions to make there and all the time to reflect on the most trivial things.

Here, I am gaining an enormous amount of knowledge, and trying to process everything which can become a bit overwhelming.

Rowan has continued my training with a bow and arrow, and Lynet is showing me how to bake. I can now make basic bread and a few different types of stews, which are delicious, if I do say so myself.

Joy is teaching me to garden, and I have planted the first seeds in a garden behind our house. I enjoy feeling the dirt beneath my hands and spent hours in the garden the first day, picking weeds and making trenches.

My favorite thing to do, though, is help in the animal stables. The village has two horses, twenty goats, thirty-two sheep, four pigs, and forty-five chickens. I walk to the other side of town every morning to place food in the troughs and freshen the water.

The first time I laid a hand on one of the horses' noses and felt that velvety skin, my entire childhood came rushing back, and I sobbed like a child as the horse nuzzled my face.

I let myself grieve for my missed childhood among the sweet hay and open stalls. While I love Rowan and confide in him about most things, a small part of me needs this part of my healing to be done alone.

The animals nuzzle me with their soft fur and gentle breath, listening in that silent, patient way that animals can.

Although not all aspects of the animals have been comforting.

Last week, I walked into the chicken coop to find a mother hen pecking at her unhatched chicks. I left the coop, sobbing for the unborn chicks, and ran right to Lynet's house. She wiped the tears from my eyes and sat me down for tea.

"Not all hens have maternal instincts," she told me, her warm amber eyes staring at my splotchy face. "Some of them are just not meant to be mothers. Same as any other species."

"What if I'm like her?" I asked her, unsure if I was referring to the hen or my mother. Both seem equally heartless, and I sobbed into the napkin Lynet gave me.

"You are nothing like her."

"But how do you know? What if I don't care for my babies after they are born?"

"Do you remember when Ewin scraped his knee, and you carried him back home to bandage it? You blew on it until the stinging stopped, and he wrapped his arms around your neck."

I nodded my head.

"Well, that is what a mother is. She often puts others' needs in front of her own. You don't need to be a mother to feel those things. Either they are present, or they are not. And I already see them shining through your eyes every day."

I wrapped my arms around her and squeezed while my tears dry. "Thank you, Lynet. For everything."

Now, feeling the babies kick inside me, I know she is right. My heart is already connected to them by an invisible string that defies logic. I won't treat them like my mother treated me. They will have every ounce of love I have to give and more. When Rowan lays next to me at night and strokes my stomach, my heart aches. It feels like my heart is breaking open but not from fear or anxiety any longer. It is bursting with love, something I didn't know was possible.

Every day my fear diminishes, replaced by a contentment that makes me feel whole. That flicker of light that was burning when I was my mother's prisoner has erupted into an inferno that shines brighter than the sun. My life here in the Darkest Woods is everything I could have dreamed of and more. These trees truly are magical and have helped heal me with their swaying branches and silent observations. Perhaps the Green Man truly did bless them. Rowan has a book of myths surrounding this mysterious man and I devour every word I can find about him.

Reading has become my favorite hobby and I spend countless hours by the fireplace transported to the worlds inside those books. Reading is not the only thing I have learned since coming here.

My world has undoubtedly expanded to new horizons, and I take everything in stride and learn as much as possible. All these newfound skills help heal my broken spirit and make me feel that same thirst for life I had as a child.

When I discover a new skill or taste a new food, everything in my universe comes to a standstill as I soak in the unique experience.

This also contributes to my indecisive nature since the possibilities are often endless. The first time Rowan noticed this, I was standing by the table with a can of jam in one hand and a plate of butter in the other. I must have been looking at them for a full two minutes before he cleared his throat, and I looked up to find him staring at me with raised brows.

"I can't decide what to have on my toast," I said, staring back and forth between the two items.

"Have them both," he suggested.

So, I did, and that is how I found out that toast with butter and jam is my very favorite food in the world. Something about that salty, sweet mixture sets my tastebuds alight and makes my mouth water.

But now, standing in our house, I know there is a decision to make. And a rather important one.

"I have to go back to the castle," I say, turning to face him.

Rowan's muscles tighten, but he doesn't utter a word. I wrap my arms around his neck and twirl the ends of his hair in my fingers. He wears it longer than he used to and the stubble on his face has grown out, giving his youthful face a rugged edge. He told me he wanted to shave it but I insisted that it suits him.

"Not for good. Just to set things right with the servants. And also..." I pause, not sure how to voice my concerns. "I need to see her in the dungeon."

I have had nightmares about my time there. It's like my unconscious can't believe it is truly over. If I see her with my own eyes locked up behind those bars, it might give me a measure of comfort from these haunting thoughts. At least, I hope it will.

"All right. But I want to bring a few of the hunters. We don't know if those creatures are gone, and we can't be too safe until we know for certain."

I kiss him lightly. "All right. Can we go soon?"

"We can go tomorrow if you like."

Nodding my head, I try to ignore the nervous tremors racing through my body.

The following day, we leave at first light. It is a few hours' walk, and we pack the necessities to tide us over for the trip. I love that Rowan doesn't coddle me despite my pregnancy. He wants me to feel strong so he treats me accordingly. He doesn't tell me I can't walk the distance but he does pack extra provisions just in case.

Then, in the chilly morning air, we set off for Cachtice Castle.

Chapter 23.

The castle is not nearly as sinister as I remember it. Before, it seemed to pulse with an invisible energy. But now, everything seems eerily still and silent. No crows adorn the fences. No beasts lurk in the shadows. Just a large stone building in the middle of the forest. Dried leaves from the previous fall crunch under our boots as we walk to the main entrance, but that is the only sound beside the trilling of the birds.

I stand in front of the main doors with a large bronze knocker debating what to do. I haven't stood in this spot for over ten years and am suddenly unsure if coming back was the right thing to do. Should I knock? Or just enter? This is silly, I decide and push the large doors open and walk inside.

The air inside smells stale like no one has occupied the space for a decade, even though it has only been six months.

"Hello," I call out. My voice rebounds off the walls and returns to me unanswered.

I walk through the entrance and go through room after room before coming across another person.

In the kitchen, Olivia is stirring a pot of soup over the stove. When we walk in, she looks up, shocked. She places a hand over her mouth when she sees that it is me. The spoon in her hand clatters to the floor as she runs to me.

In all my years here, she has never hugged me, but now, she embraces me so tightly that I fear she will break my bones.

The joy on her face makes my heart hurt, and a tear rolls down her face when she looks into my eyes.

"I'm so sorry," she says. "So sorry for not helping you all those years or finding a way for you to escape. I have waited a long time to tell you this, and now I am making a mess of it."

She blows her nose into a handkerchief as her tears begin to flow freely.

"You were kinder to me than anyone. She would have found me if you had helped me escape, and things would have been much worse for you. Please don't fret. Things turned out all right in the end. Didn't they?"

"Oh yes," she agrees, nodding vigorously. "I have been feeding her some bread and soup every day, but that is all. At first, she screamed at me and said she would do horrible things but the last few months she has quieted down. She seems to have accepted her fate."

Guilt gnaws at me that I left Olivia to deal with her alone, but I swallow it down for the time being and take Olivia's hands in mine. "I need to see her. Just one last time."

"Of course. I understand."

"But first, I need you all to help me with something."

Rowan cocks his eye and grins. "What do you have up your sleeve, Little Bird?"

"I'll show you," I say with a half-smile.

"Do you need more help?" Olivia asks. "I have another servant here with me. He helps me take care of the castle since everyone else left."

A faint blush spreads over Olivia's cheeks, and I fight to keep down a grin.

"He?"

She casts her eyes to the ground and whispers, "Joshua."

"Yes, please. See if Joshua will be willing to help. This may take us a while."

We begin walking up the stairs when I stop with one hand on the railing. "Wait." I say turning to Olivia. "What is your real name? All these years I have called you Olivia in my head."

Her eyes glitter and her lips quirk up into a smile. "It's Jessica."

"Jessica. That suits you." I will have a hard time coming to terms with this new name. In my head I chant Jessica repeatedly, trying to imprint it over the familiar Olivia which has resided there for so long.

We walk through the castle, and I point out objects to collect. One by one, we bring the items downstairs and throw them onto a pile. Mirrors and pictures. Goblets and hair brushes. Anything that reminds me of my mother is added to the growing pile. Nearly everything in her bedroom except her bed is moved since it is too heavy. Magda's potions, herbs, and horrible mortar and pestle are also added. Everything is dropped unceremoniously onto the heap.

The vial containing my father's spirit winks at me when I pass it, and I pick it up to examine it. It may be foolish because who knows what the vial contains, but I uncork it and watch the blue orb float out of the bottle. It hovers in the air for a few minutes before whirling around my body and shooting off into the sky.

I'd like to think that if that were indeed my father's soul, he would be happy to be free and out of the clutches of my mother.

The only object I keep is an oak spinning wheel which we find in the servants' quarters and covered with dust. I run my fingers over the smooth wheel and can already picture it in the corner of our little home.

After an entire afternoon of hauling items, we take a break to rest and have a bite to eat.

Olivia... I mean Jessica.... makes us delicious tomato soup and warm bread smeared with thick butter.

While she is cleaning up and the others are bringing down a few heavier objects, I make my way to the dungeon.

Walking down the stairs is like walking down memory lane in the worst possible way. Every step makes me feel smaller than the previous one until I might be no taller than a mouse, ready to scuttle under the nearest rock. The time I spent here had begun to feel so far away, but now the familiar sights and smells bring it to the forefront of my mind. My mind will always try to erase the time I spent here but it will never truly be gone. When you go through something like this it sticks with you forever, branding you with an invisible scar that remains inside you forever.

I reach the threshold and try to unclench my teeth before entering. After everything I have experienced over the last six months, it makes my existence here seem even more miserable. But I throw back my shoulders, wipe away a tear that escaped my eye, and march forward. When I reach my old room, my stomach turns to jelly facing the place where she imprisoned me for nearly ten years.

The key to the cell is hanging next to the door, just where Olivia told me it would be. Picking it up, I clutch it tightly, trying to make my fingers stop trembling. I lay a hand on my protruding stomach and steady my breathing.

I am not that girl anymore and refuse to cower.

With that thought, I open the cell.

My mother is sitting in the corner of the bed, rocking back and forth and muttering under her breath.

The mirror I gave her is on the bed next to her, and she picks it up every few seconds to investigate the reflection before placing it back on the bed. I watch for a few minutes while she repeats this process.

She doesn't turn to acknowledge my presence. She mutters to herself, just under her breath. I take another deep breath and step further into the room. Her gaze swings to me when I am within a few feet of her. Her once luxurious hair is now stringy and thin. The alabaster skin she was so proud of is mottled with red, and wrinkles are beginning to crease that once unblemished surface.

She would be horrified by the image she presents if she had her wits about her. She reaches down to itch at the skin on her legs, and when she lifts the hem of her dirty dress, I see raw skin from where she has scraped it away with her fingernails.

"The bugs. They are trying to burrow under my flesh. I won't let them, though," she cackles. "I catch and eat them before they burrow under my skin."

She picks at an imaginary bug on her leg and places it on her tongue. Closing her eyes, she relishes the taste before shifting her bloodshot eyes back to me.

A brief recognition flares in her eyes but retreats a moment later. It appears she has gone completely mad. Where is the woman who reigned chaos on so many people for most of her life? She has completely lost her mind after only a few months in this cell. The realization that I survived in an environment where she cannot gives me a strange amount of satisfaction. I survived what she could not. I am stronger than she is.

I had wanted to come here to say my peace. Tell her exactly how I feel about her and what she did to me. But looking at this husk of a woman, I realize that I don't care about defending myself to her. Nothing I can say to her will matter, and nothing she says to me will change anything for me. It won't change who I am now or what my future holds. I hold the power now. That revelation causes one side of my mouth to lift. This chapter of my life is over, and I will never set eyes on this woman again. At least not while she is alive.

"Goodbye, Mother," I say with a sigh.

She returns to her rocking and pays no attention as I walk from the cell. On the way out, I see my old mask hanging from that same nail on the inside of the doorframe. I grab it and lock the door behind me.

When I return to the main entrance of the castle, everyone is standing around the giant mound of items we compiled.

"Are you ready?" Rowan asks, with that lopsided grin I love so much.

I stand on my tiptoes and kiss him.

The mask cracks in two when it lands on the pile and I wrap my arms around Rowan's waist.

"I'm ready."

He strikes a match and hands it to me. The flame flickers in the wind but remains lit when I throw it on top of the heap. The first thing that begins to burn is the portrait of my mother with the man's decapitated head. The fabric melts as the heat intensifies until the last pieces curl up and fall into the heap. It doesn't take long for the rest of the pile to turn into an inferno, and I watch as every piece of Elizabeth's legacy goes up in flames.

Olivia... I mean Jessica…. Damn it. I almost wish I hadn't asked her real name… walks over to me and throws an arm around my shoulders as we watch the fire burn. Her cheeks are rosy from the heat, and we step back to distance ourselves from the blaze.

"A solicitor came by a few weeks ago, asking about Elizabeth. He was told by one of the servants who left that she was deceased, and I did nothing to discredit his information. He said that as the only heir, Castle Cachtice and all of Elizabeth's possessions will transfer to you."

This information sinks in, and I contemplate what this means for me.

It doesn't change anything. For now, I will do nothing.

Gazing at this large gothic building, I feel no urge to reinsert myself into this life.

"Will you keep it up for a while?" I ask Jessica. "You can hire more staff if needed. There should be more than enough money for wages in mothers' coffers."

"Joshua and I can manage," she replies, blushing.

Oh, I'm sure they will do more than manage. I clasp her hands in mine, and we watch piece after piece dissolve into glowing embers.

I will need time to determine what to do with the castle. Maybe I will keep it. Maybe I will sell it. Or maybe one day I will return and burn the whole thing to the ground.

The end.

Acknowledgments

I would like to thank everyone who has made this book possible.

To my children, who have had unlimited patience with my writing and editing at all hours of the day and night.

To my sisters, who were my sounding board during the writing process and also the first people to read my book.

To my oldest son who gave me invaluable advice to the overall storyline and plot details.

To the beta readers I used who gave me feedback on the plot and editing suggestions.

To my editor, who was infinitely patient with my questions and the additional feedback she delivered with her work.

Most of all to my husband, who has spent the last few months listening to me work through every obstacle and give me suggestions on how to overcome them to achieve this dream.

Thank you all for letting me lean on you.

Printed in Great Britain
by Amazon

42165738R00175